To my children, Sebastian, Alex and Cole;
And to my granddaughter, Sabrina Rose,
Who inspire me daily with their intelligence and love;

And to the memory of my husband, Allan—
Who always made the world beautiful for me.

THE FLOWER GIRLS
By Susan Thaler

PART ONE: BLUE SKIES

Chapter 1
DAISY

She knew there was a reason she should get out of bed, but she was still so sleepy, so comfortable beneath the covers. But Pip was twitching in his sleep again, pulling her to wakefulness.

It was funny to see Pip's paws moving as he lay on his back, as though he were dreaming about running. Poor Pip had never run in his entire life, unless you counted sprinting from the bedroom into the kitchen for his dinner. There was hardly enough space to walk, much less run, in their tiny apartment, and naturally he wasn't allowed Outside.

The thought of Pip accidentally escaping to Outside was enough to wake her fully. She opened her eyes to the day's weak light filtering through the window shade.

"Rose? Violet?" She checked her sisters' floor mats. Empty. Then she remembered: Today was Domes-Day! Violet had probably gone to one of her meetings in protest of the celebration as usual. "Celebrate *what*?" Violet asked loudly in last night's argument. "They open the Dome for a few minutes to make us think we're breathing real air and then they close it again because they say Outside is still polluted! How do we really know? We *don't* know! They're just lying to us—"

"Violet!" their father had warned, "Lower your voice!" He was afraid she would be heard by the neighbors, and then someone would file a complaint and Violet would accrue another 10 points on her record for being unpatriotic. Fifty points and she'd have to go for another round of retraining—a week in S.T.E.P. Juvey—and miss school. Daisy didn't know for sure, but Violet probably had close to 50 points on her record already. The thought of her sister going back to that horrible place was frightening. There were rumors that being sent to a Save The Earth Police retraining camp more than once could rob a person of their sanity.

Daisy shuddered and threw off the covers. Pip whimpered. "Wake up, Pippy! If I have to get up, so do you!"

She tiptoed into the bathroom in case her mom was still asleep. All the schools were closed for Domes-Day and she didn't want to wake her mother on the rare day that she could sleep past six o'clock. Her mom was looking so tired lately, and Daisy was concerned, even though her father assured her that it was nothing to worry about. "She's getting older, that's all," her father had said. "I've checked her out and your mother's fine."

Of course, the fact that she was "getting older" in itself was something to worry about. After age 60, the Centers for Population Control required you to go for yearly screenings to determine Relevance. After age 65, you had to go every six months. But her mother hadn't even reached 55 yet, so Daisy guessed there was no real need to worry. Not yet, anyway.

In the bathroom she pushed the button on the shower wall for hot water. It never was actually hot, just barely warm. It would run warm for almost two full minutes, and then it would turn ice cold. This time, it ran warm for only about half a minute, which meant that both her sisters and probably her mother and father as well had already showered. Well, it was her own fault; she should have gotten up much earlier. But she'd been dreaming about Sharkey Collins again. They were in history class together this year. She'd had a crush on him forever: Blonde wavy hair and a deep dimple in his chin. And when he smiled... Daisy sighed. What was the use? A boy like Sharkey Collins would never be interested in a girl like her, a *Waster*. He'd even called her that once when they were in elementary school. Her face burned at the memory.

When she'd changed into her Domes-Day outfit—red tee, white scarf, blue shorts—she found Rose and her mother at the kitchen table, arguing quietly. You had to speak softly in this apartment because the walls were made of Neufab, a kind of hardened paste that was supposed to resemble wood. All the buildings here in Blue Skies Dome were constructed of it, as there was no real wood anywhere on the planet that she knew of. All the trees had either died or been swept out to sea in the first few years of the Warming.

"You're the only one in the family who wants to do this!" Rose said petulantly. "Going Pioneer is a crazy idea!"

"It is *not* crazy! And I am not the only one: Violet agrees with me!" her mother whispered harshly. They were seated at the tiny round kitchen table, their breakfast wafers lying untouched on their plates. "I'm begging you to just give it some thought..."

"Good morning," Daisy said. "And a happy Domes-Day to you."

"What's happy about it?" Rose said, standing, her chair scraping noisily against the mock marble floor. She gave Daisy an imploring look. "See if you can talk some sense into her."

Rose was wearing the same Domes-Day outfit that Daisy had on, but on her it looked incredibly glamorous. It was no secret that Rose was the real beauty in the family, with her long red hair and perfect figure. She would probably have been voted Most Beautiful Earth Queen at school if she had been allowed to enter the contest. But of course, being a triplet (*Waster!*), she was ineligible.

Daisy frowned. She was tired of being caught in the middle of this argument about going Pioneer: Violet pulling her one way, Rose the other, their mother aligned with Violet, their father with Rose.

"Daisy, fix yourself some breakfast, honey. It's getting late." Her mother smiled. Beneath the smile Daisy could see how weary she was.

"I'll see you at the Sector 4 parade area," Rose said. "Don't be late."

"When have I ever been late for Domes-Day?" Daisy said with annoyance. It was a rhetorical question. Rose slammed the door behind her without saying goodbye.

She was off to meet Decker Bliss, Daisy knew. They were both scheduled to march in the parade, and Deck was going to give one of the speeches for Earth Unity. It was a huge honor, given only to those who had done their utmost during the year to protect the earth's resources. What was left of them, anyway.

Daisy felt jealous. Decker was such a cool boyfriend. Not as handsome as Sharkey Collins, perhaps, but wonderful all the same. He was sweet and kind and he came from one of the most respected families in Blue Skies Dome. He was totally in love with Rose, and the fact that she was a triplet didn't even seem to matter.

Chapter 2
ROSE

Decker was already at the parade post when she arrived. Naturally. He was never late for anything. This should have pleased her—he was so considerate and thoughtful and, well, *perfect*—but today for some reason his punctuality annoyed her. She had started the day off on the wrong foot, arguing with her mother again about the same, stupid subject: Moving out of Blue Skies for an unknown Pioneer district. What an incredibly dumb idea!

"Hi," she practically sneered at Deck. "Sorry I'm late."

He looked at her. "Hi, yourself, and you're not late. What's wrong?"

That was another thing: Deck could read her moods perfectly. He always knew when something was bothering her. "Nothing," she said, "nothing's wrong," and gave him a quick peck on the cheek.

The parade area was crowding up quickly. Rose was jostled by a group of marchers who were in a hurry to get to the front of the line, and she yelled, "Hey, watch it!" to a boy when his baton hit her hip.

"Watch it yourself, freak!" he yelled back.

"Hey!" Decker called, moving towards him.

Rose blocked his way. "Forget it," she said, and kissed him more convincingly, on the lips this time.

The parade would start in a matter of minutes. There was no time for a fight. "I don't know how you tolerate it," he said, hugging her. She rested her head against him, and heard his heart beating rapidly inside his chest. "Dumb *Fossil Fueler*!" Decker mumbled.

Rose looked up at him, surprised. It was the worst insult anyone could give to another human. People who used fossil fuels—coal, gas, oil—were blamed for the Warming, not caring that those fuels released more carbon dioxide into the atmosphere than Earth could absorb; wrapping the world in a noxious blanket of unbearable heat.

"I just ignore them," she said. She wanted to add, "I'm so used to it." But if she said it, he might think she was asking for pity, and she would never want that.

It wasn't her fault that she was a triplet. Her parents didn't know until almost the moment she was born that there would be three babies instead of two. Evidently she had been hiding behind Violet in the womb. Or maybe behind Daisy. No one really knew.

Two babies would have been bad enough. The CPC one-child-only rule was usually inviolable. And it was understandable, what with the near depletion of Earth's resources; water, food, the very air itself, were in very short supply. Whatever remained of the planet could not sustain too many humans. It was as simple—and as complicated—as that.

Her father had been prepared to pay the government the standard extra fee—$50,000—for the twins that were expected. Dad was a valuable asset to Blue Skies—to the planet as a whole, really, because dedicated doctors, like the earth's resources, were in short supply. So their family was permitted to override the one-child-only law. But a third baby? A *triplet*? The Board of Presidents themselves would have been denied that privilege.

But her father had refused to murder his child for the benefit of society. "What if she grows up to find a way to make the oceans recede? Or to resurrect the Ice Shelf? Or if she finds a way to reforest Africa? No, I refuse to discard a potential Saver!"

Her mother said that if her baby would not be allowed to live, she might kill herself as well.

Suicide was still considered morally wrong 16 years ago. To this day, Rose wasn't sure her mother wouldn't have made good on her threat. They never discussed this at home, of course. The very subject was forbidden.

In the end, her father paid a total of $100,000 to the CPC to allow Rose to stay born. In addition, he had to promise to remain a practicing physician in Blue Skies for the rest of his life, and never, under any circumstances, go Pioneer.

Had her mother forgotten about that promise? Rose wondered. How could she ask the family to become Pioneers and leave Blue Skies when she knew it would never be allowed?

Rose followed Decker to the area where the parade would start any minute now. They would march from here throughout the entire sector—a total of four miles.

After that, the speeches would begin, including the one Deck would give for Earth Unity. She was so proud of him!

She wished again that she could tell him about the dissension in her family, about her mother's crazy desire to leave domed security. But she couldn't risk it. If he knew there was even a remote chance that her family might relocate, he might slip and tell his parents, who were strict Domers. Rose and her family would be open to ridicule and called Yearners or something equally offensive.

And worst of all: If they left, she would never see Decker again. The thought made her want to cry.

"Rose! Rose! Over here!" She looked up at the bleachers that lined the parade route and saw Daisy waving to her.

Rose waved back. The music was starting up. She and Decker stepped out together, swinging their arms rhythmically to the uplifting music of "This Land of Hope", one of her favorite songs. Later, after the speeches, there would be the Opening of the Dome, the most solemn moment of the whole year. It was rumored the Dome might stay open for a whole five minutes this year!

Her parents were somewhere in the crowd, too. Everyone who mattered to her was here. Everyone except Violet, that is. But she wouldn't let Violet's absence upset her. Not today.

She turned to Decker. He smiled at her and she smiled back. They marched in perfect rhythm, shoulder to shoulder, side by side. Which was exactly where she wanted to be. Side by side with Deck. Forever and ever.

Chapter 3

VIOLET

They watched the Opening of the Dome in silence. The ugly brown SumbraSteel doors parted, and a narrow column of gray sky slowly came into view. The crowd roared. "We can see it! We can see it! Look! The sky!" they yelled, jumping and waving and hugging each another. A few crazed souls actually fell out of the bleachers in their excitement.

"Idiots," Violet said in disgust. "Turn it off!"

"Hey, I wanna watch!" Clinker James said. "I wanna see the skyyyyy!" he mimicked, dissolving into derisive laughter.

"Yeah, me too," said Bloo Sycamore, crossing her eyes and pretending to lose her balance. "Oh, no, I'm falling! The air still sucks! Someone catch me!" And she slid onto the fake earth floor of their meeting room.

"Not funny," Violet said. "They're being fooled and they don't even know it." She tapped the holograph button and the room went quiet. The sudoflickers lit up and the shabby headquarters of the Truth Be Told Alliance became visible.

"Maybe we're *not* being lied to," said Brink Trayor. "D'ja ever think of that?" He looked up from the pile of flyers on his desk. "Maybe the air *is* still unfit to breathe..."

Everyone stared at him. When Violet realized that he was being serious, she frowned. "Come on, Brink! It's been over 200 years! In all that time the air Outside must have become habitable—at least in some places, at least here, in the States—in the Pacific Northwest! My mom said..."

"Your mom? Excuse me, Violet, but everyone knows your mom is—" he stopped short.

Violet's jaw tightened. "My mom is what? *Crazy?* Go on, say it!"

Brink stood up, his 6'7" frame towering above her. "She had *triplets* for Dome's sake! That's not exactly what a sane person would do!"

"Brink!" Bloo gasped, shocked. "That's enough!"

"Yeah, man, that was uncalled for!" said Clinker.

To her horror, Violet found herself tearing up. "So you're saying my sister, Rose, should never have been born? That she should have been discarded?"

Brink moved closer to her. "Not discarded, just—" He shrugged. "How come your mother didn't get pregnant the normal way, like most people?"

Violet stared at him. Could he really be that stupid? "She *did* get pregnant the normal way, you dope! Getting injected with CPC chemicals is *abnormal*!"

Brink shook his head and looked confused. But then he reached for her and she let herself be drawn into his arms. "I'm sorry, Vi, I'm so sorry...I don't know what's the matter with me. I was up half the night getting the flyers ready, and I think my dad's getting suspicious because I catch him watching me every minute and—"

"It was 16 years ago," Violet interrupted. "That time when the CPC's fertility chemicals were sabotaged! Did you forget? All the fetuses kept dying until they found the poisoned batch. My mom didn't want that happening to her baby." She paused. "*Babies*." She gave him a sad smile. "Hey, don't you pay attention in Recent History class? My mom said she thought you were always daydreaming!"

"Yeah," Brink chuckled. "Daydreaming about you!"

That night they distributed the flyers under cover of darkness. Not one sudoflicker was on anywhere, not even in the S.T.E.P. building, which was always lit up day and night, all year long. But tonight, even the Save The Earth Police were probably stuporous from drinking Newcohol on this most solemn holiday.

Well, at least another Domes-Day was over, Violet thought as she slipped the last Truth Be Told flyer under the last apartment door.

It was their most attractive flyer ever. Titled "The Way Things Used to Be," it contained photos of people walking around Outside with no Dome overhead! There were pictures of forests and rivers and animals like polar bears. Violet's mother had loaned them to her for the flyers. "Be careful with these," her mother had said. "They're very valuable."

"I will, Mom," Violet assured her. And she had been.

Her mother's photo archive must be the most expansive in the entire world, Violet thought as she walked toward their apartment now in the darkness, careful not to make a sound. It was well past curfew, and she couldn't risk another stint in S.T.E.P. Juvey. The mere thought made her tremble.

Other Yearners—that's what they called people who were yearning to breathe free—had good photo collections, too—but none were as well preserved as her mom's. She and her mom had spent countless hours looking at the pictures of how life used to be before the Warming obliterated most of the planet.

"It all happened, so quickly," her mom told her. "The scientists tried to persuade people how imminent the Warming was, but no one believed them. Some even thought such a catastrophe could never happen—or that if it did, it would probably take a thousand years or so before things got really bad."

"A thousand years?!" Violet gasped. "But didn't things start to get bad really fast—in 2055, right? Didn't the temperature go above 160°F for the first time in— what was it—February of that year? In Florida? That was only a little over 200 years ago!"

Her mother nodded. Violet saw how sad she looked. It always ended that way—with her mom tearing up at the thought of all that had been lost in this once beautiful world.

Everyone was asleep when Violet let herself into the apartment. She found her way to her mat without waking either Rose or Daisy. Pip whimpered slightly from his place on Daisy's mat but luckily he didn't wake up.

That night Violet dreamed they had fled to a Pioneer area and were greeted by polar bears. The bears stood in a welcoming circle, their fur gleaming white in the clear, unpolluted air. Even in the dream she knew she was dreaming because ever since the Arctic ice had melted and the oceans had risen to unimaginable heights, polar bears had vanished from Planet Earth.

Chapter 4
SUNELLEN

The stack of test papers on her desk was daunting. This was the essay test she gave at the end of every year and it counted for half her students' grade. She had given them a choice of three topics:

1. "The History of the Doming in the United States"
2. "Recovery: A Best-Case Scenario for Planet Earth"
3. "Pioneering—For or Against. Discuss"

She knew that most would choose the first topic, about Doming, because it was easy to research and didn't require much independent thought. The next most popular subject would be their ideas for the Recovery, when it would come (if it came at all, she thought morosely) and the likelihood of permanence.

She thought Daisy would probably choose this option. Daisy always sought the middle ground. She wouldn't want to alienate Rose by being for leaving Blue Skies for Pioneering; and she wouldn't want to alienate Violet by being against it.

As for the third choice—the idea of leaving a secure domed environment to explore the unknowable—well, Sunellen would be surprised if even one student would tackle that one.

The idea was very controversial, with half the population under the Domes claiming it was near treason to want to defect to an unknown, possibly inhabitable world, and the other half saying it was foolish not to explore other options. What if the Pioneers were right and the world was slowly being nursed back to health by courageous souls willing to die to find out? There was no way to know for sure, of course, since no form of communication could penetrate the SumbraSteel of any Dome.

Teenagers, she knew, tended to avoid problematic subjects (except, of course, Violet, who was the epitome of controversy).

"They're brainwashed," Sunellen's friend, Terra Brown, said the last time they talked about it. "They believe what their parents preach." The thought of Terra brought a pang of jealousy. The Browns had applied for Pioneering and were pretty certain of getting permission to leave Blue Skies. After all, Terra's husband hadn't made any promises to stay for a lifetime, Sunellen thought.

And Terra hadn't made the mistake of having triplets...

Not that Sunellen thought of her girls as a mistake. They were the best things in her life. She loved each one with all her heart. And Prentiss, too. She loved him as much today as when they first met in EcoCulture class all those years ago. She sighed. If only he would *consider* asking for a release from his promise. But he could be so stubborn!

"Sunellen? How late will you be staying today?" Mr. Collins, the principal, was smiling at her from the doorway. It was not a genuine smile; more like a grimace.

"I'll be leaving in a nanosec," she said. She hadn't realized it was so late; the sudoflickers were still lit, and it was nearly close-out time. Mr. Collins was very strict about not wasting light. He was a go-by-the-rules kind of guy. Boring and finicky and not the sort of boss she would have preferred working for. He was also Sharkey Collins's father.

Sharkey was very popular—handsome in an All-American way with his blonde wavy hair and dimpled chin. But he was a lazy student, and beneath his dazzling smile she detected a prejudicial streak. She remembered that years ago, when he and Daisy were in the same class in elementary school, he had whispered *"Waster"* at her. It had broken Sunellen's heart to see Daisy cry about that, and she wanted to rip Sharkey's head off, but of course she'd done no such thing. She'd thought then, as now, that children usually reflected the views of their parents.

What was that wonderful expression from before the Warming? *The apple doesn't fall far from the tree?* It was a beautiful expression. How glorious would it be to see a living tree laden with real fruit! Her grandparents had told her about the trees. There had been so many kinds: elm, maple, and trees called pine that had a beautiful fragrance. Was that the kind of tree people cut down to bring into their homes in order to celebrate Christmas? she wondered. She believed it was.

Her eyes filled with tears. Imagine killing a live tree just for decoration! Since deforestation, no one alive now had ever seen a real tree. She had memorized most of their names: magnolia, cherry, dogwood, apple. No one she knew had ever tasted an apple. A *real* apple, anyway. The apple wafers made by the Simulated Food Centers were supposedly grown from seeds that had been salvaged before the Domes were erected, but she doubted they bore any resemblance to the real thing.

Sunellen stuffed the pile of exam papers into her briefcase and flicked out the lights. She would read them tonight, after dinner, if she could stay awake that long. This feeling of fatigue wasn't going away, and it worried her. But she wouldn't think about that now. She preferred to think about the trees and their beautiful names.

Chapter 5

DAISY

Her watch pinged softly. Daisy glanced at her wrist and Calla's face appeared within the crystal circle. Calla looked excited. "Meet me after class in the garden!" her caption read. "I've got good news!"

Daisy's shoulders sagged. *Oh, no,* she thought. Please, please, no. She knew what Calla was going to say. And from Daisy's standpoint, the news was definitely not going to be good.

Daisy almost always knew what was going to happen before it even happened. Her parents tried to convince her that this was a gift and she should cherish it. "Use it wisely," her father advised, adding: "It used to be known as precognition, and is still very rare. Research has shown it might have something to do with overdevelopment of the prefrontal cortex..."

She had tuned him out. Today they called it The Knowing, and it was just another thing that made her seem different from everyone else.

Maybe I'm wrong this time, Daisy hoped. Once or twice in the past she had been wrong, like the time when she felt sure that her dog, Pip, would escape to Outside and she'd never see him again. Thank Dome that hadn't happened.

"Daisy—Daisy Budd! Are we boring you?"

Daisy looked up to find the entire class staring at her. Mr. Moonrock was frowning. He always seemed to be frowning.

Daisy shifted uncomfortably in her seat. "Could you please repeat the question, sir?"

The class snickered. She thought she heard someone whisper, "Stupid Waster," but it was probably her imagination. Or not.

"I asked you what caused the intertropical convergence zone to shift southward and what happened as a result! Or did you not bother to study the passage I assigned to the class yesterday?"

Daisy stood, her face burning. "I—I'm sorry, but no—I mean, yes, I did study, but—" She cleared her throat. "The intertropical convergence zone shifted southward because of the simultaneous warming of the south and the cooling of the north. This worsened the droughts in North Africa and the whole region lost 30 percent of its precipitation."

Mr. Moonrock allowed a hint of a smile to replace his default frown. Then he pointed to Ellis Starr to continue the saga of the destruction and death of an entire continent.

Calla was waiting for her in the garden after school. It wasn't a real garden, of course, because no plants or trees or anything truly alive could flourish under SumbraSteel, no matter how hard the scientists tried. And they *had* tried. Multitudes of seeds had been developed and placed in all kinds of different soils over the years, each one promising at first. Occasionally, teeny green sprouts might poke up from the newest plantings, but, inevitably, fail to thrive. There was a reward of $100,000,000 and free food wafers for life if any botanist could develop a genuine, living, chemically free plant.

So the garden had been "planted" with NewBloom stalks (green plastic stems with wafer-like colored circles on top) that were supposed to have a sweet fragrance, but that actually smelled like rubber. Around them, holograms of the real thing—fields of trees and flowers and lakes from before the Warming—covered the circular walls.

Calla waved to her from a bench near a circle of NewBlooms. "You'll never guess!" she whispered excitedly as Daisy sat down beside her. "We were approved!"

Luckily, they were the only people at this end of the garden, or Calla might have been overheard. Leaving Blue Skies (or any other Domed sector) for a Pioneer area, while still not illegal, was also not really approved of. There had been instances of Yearners' apartments being trashed and—this was the worst part for Daisy—any pets to be found were tossed Outside where they would meet a horrible fate.

"Oh, Calla," Daisy sighed, tears filling her eyes. "I'm so happy for you. But—"

Calla leaned over and hugged her. "Really? You don't look very happy," she teased. "I know, Daze. I'll miss you, too. You're the best friend I ever had! But maybe your family will join us later! You said your mom and Violet aren't exactly happy here!"

Daisy shook her head. Most everyone knew about her father's obligation to remain in Blue Skies forever, Calla included.

"Maybe they'll release him," Calla said. "Your dad's been their best doctor for over 30 years! Maybe they don't need him as much as they once did..."

Daisy shook her head. "My dad says people are still getting sick and he's been compelled to send more and more people to Relevance. The Board of Presidents will never let my dad leave! I know it!"

They sat in silence for a moment. Daisy forced herself to ask: "When do you think you'll be leaving Blue Skies?"

Calla sighed. "They haven't told us yet. They leave that for last. We have to be ready to go at a moment's notice."

Daisy asked, "Are you scared?"

"A little. But excited, too. Whatever's out there can't be much worse than here. At least, I hope not."

"My mom's going to be really upset," Daisy said. She and your mom are like sisters."

"I know, but—" Before she could finish, a chime sounded and the sudoflickers flickered their last dim light for the day. The NewBloom stalks folded into tiny blobs and disappeared into the fake grass. The beautiful scenes of trees and flowers and lakes faded from the walls, leaving the Garden looking stark and ominous.

"We'd better go," Daisy said. And, "You're taking Digger, right?"

"Of course!" Calla said. "We're gonna give him a shot of DremeSoFine so he'll stay asleep during the trip, like the rules say."

Digger and Pip came from the same litter. They had nearly identical markings: gray body, white curly tail and matching white triangular shaped ears. Daisy and Calla had found them one day about a year ago as they walked home from school. The pups had been chained behind a thick length of tubing at a defunct desalination center several blocks from their apartment sector. Someone had been planning to bring them to a Relevance Lab where they would be—Daisy shuddered, unable to finish the thought.

"Are they real?" Calla had asked, picking one puppy up and cuddling it against her chest.

"Of course they're real!" Daisy exclaimed. "No Robotron could be this adorable!" She picked up the other puppy and brought it close to her face, inhaling its sweet, doggy scent. She'd known a few people who had pets but never actually held one. Its fur was softer than anything she'd ever imagined.

"I'm keeping him!" both girls said at exactly the same time. They giggled and hooked pinkies. It was a gesture that was supposed to bring good luck.

Remembering this, Daisy thought their good luck had finally run out. This could be the last time she would see Calla. Or it might be tomorrow, or the day after.

"Bye, Calla, see you soon," Daisy said now, as her tears turned the whole world into a blur.

Chapter 6

A SAMPLE ESSAY

*Recent Ancient History, Mrs. Budd
June 15, 2275*

THE HISTORY OF THE DOMING OF THE UNITED STATES

By Sharkey Collins

The first Domes were erected in 2073 in the Southern part of the United States in order to filter out the air pollution created by greenhouse gases when the Warming got out of control.

The early Domes didn't do so well, as SumbraSteel hadn't been invented yet, and the material they used at first didn't prevent the carbon dioxide from seeping in and killing crops and humans.

After SumbraSteel, things on Earth got a lot better. It took a long time— approximately 30 years—to erect all the

Domes. It was a very expensive project to create the Domes, as they had to provide total protection for every human being in our great country. But after experimenting with all kinds of materials like NoPol metals and Xcarb02 which kept either cracking or leaking, the scientists finally came up with SumbraSteel which is totally great. Even though we have to pay a lot of taxes to keep the Domes in good shape, I feel it's worth it. Now every single state has protection from the heat and tsunamis.

The biggest Domed cities are in Rainbow Arc which covers the land from Vermont to Ohio, and Clearpoint View which covers the area from Wyoming to Nevada. There are many smaller Domes in-between, and each dome contains many sectors.

Personally, I think my own dome, Blue Skies, is the best one of all. It covers 1200 miles and has many, many sectors. I live in Sector 4. Our dome hasn't leaked even once in all these years, and it provides great simulated sunlight. I bet no one could tell the difference between real sun and our wonderful Blue Skies sun.

I do not understand those Yearners who want to leave our great Domed cities for the Pioneer areas because they think Dome living isn't healthy anymore. They have the false assumption that there are some places out there in Pioneerville (ha-ha, I made that term up!) that have started to recover from the Warming. Well, if they want to go, I say, Good Riddance! But I plan to stay right here, in good ol' Blue Skies, for as long as it takes, and maybe even after that!

Chapter 7
ROSE

"This is stupid!" Rose shouted as she flung the Truth Be Told flyer onto the kitchen table. It slipped to the floor and Pip, his ears flicking up in surprise, grabbed it and shook it to and fro in his mouth. "That's right, Pip boy, chew it up!"

"Pip! Drop it!" Violet ordered, and Pip reluctantly let the flyer drop. Violet glared at her sister. "Tell me what you think is stupid about it?"

"Everything! 'The Way Things Used To Be'?" Rose wrinkled her nose. "What does that even mean? Who cares how things used to be? We're here, *now*, and that's all that matters! You could get us all in trouble with this! I can't believe Mom let you put her pictures in it! Did anyone see you distributing them? Because if they did..."

"No one saw! We—I'm—always very careful, you know that!" Violet shook her head. "You may be beautiful, Rose, but you're the most narrow-minded—"

"Enough already!" Daisy interrupted, holding her hands against her ears. "I can't take it anymore!" She looked at Violet. "Rose has a point. If S.T.E.P. catches you with these you could do another stint in Juvey..."

"No one's catching anyone," Violet said, annoyed. "And what about you, Daisy? Where do you stand on this issue? Your best friend is going Pioneer and you're still afraid to—"

"What?!" Rose interrupted, her green eyes widening. "The Browns are leaving Blue Skies?"

"How did you find out?" Daisy demanded.

Violet shrugged. "You know news travels fast in this place! That's one of the things I hate about it!"

"I can't believe it," Rose said, sitting down. "Calla Brown? A Pioneer?" And then, "Oh, no—Mom must be..."

"...Miserable," Daisy finished the sentence. "Yes. She is. I heard her crying this morning. "She'll miss Terra terribly."

"Well, I don't know about you, but that sim sun looks mighty good about now," Violet said in a mocking tone. "Daisy—why don't we take Pip for a walk Outside and see what happens?"

"Not funny!" Daisy snapped. She picked Pip up and kissed him on his round gray head. "I'll never, never ever, let you escape to Outside, darling Pip, I promise!" She turned to Rose. "I'm going to buy some Fako Chips," she said to Rose. "Will you keep an eye on him?"

Rose nodded. "Go ahead. I'm not meeting Decker until this afternoon." She took Pip from Daisy and walked with him into the living room.

Her mother had gone to the library to grade exam papers, she said, but Rose suspected she needed time to herself to mourn the imminent loss of her best friend, Terra Brown. She felt sorry for Daisy, too, who would lose *her* best friend, Calla.

"This is really bad, Pip," Rose said, massaging the dog in the space between his ears. Pip looked up at her as if to say, "Bad? Really? Okay, but keep on massaging, that feels great!"

She asked herself if it weren't for Decker, would she be so against leaving Blue Skies? Looking at her mom's photos from the time before the Warming, she admitted being curious about what it might be like to eat food that had been grown from real crops instead of the pulverized chemicals of the protein wafers.

Gently setting Pip down on the floor, she said, "I don't care. I love Decker too much to ever leave Blue Skies! We're fine right where we are, right, Pip?"

"Something's bothering you, and I'd like to know what it is," Deck said gently later that day. They were sitting on a park bench near a holograph of a waterfall. High above them, fake white clouds floated against the domed SumbraSteel ceiling. NewBloom stalks swayed gently in the breeze generated by the invisible vents that encircled them.

Rose shook her head. "I don't think I can tell you," she whispered, her eyes filling with tears.

Deck slipped his arm around her shoulders. He buried his face in her long red hair. "I love you so much," he said. "You can tell me anything, my beautiful Rosebud."

She smiled in spite of her tears. It was Deck's favorite nickname for her: *Rosebud*. "My family wants to leave Blue Skies!" she blurted. "Well, not my *entire* family. Mainly just my mom and Violet."

"But you *can't* leave—because of your father's promise!"

Rose sighed. "I know. But my father can be very persuasive," she said dryly. "Look at me; I stayed born, didn't I?" she sighed.

"That would never happen today," Decker shook his head. "The new Board of Presidents would never allow triplets. They're even cracking down on twins. I heard the price for twins now is $2,000,000. Not many families have that kind of money."

They fell silent. Suddenly, Decker blurted, "Marry me. I love you! You love me! Marry me!"

Rose stared at him, dumbstruck. "Deck! We're only sixteen! We can't get mar—"

He stopped her with a kiss. "Yes we can! We'll elope! We'll say we're 18! We'll get phony papers made up and—" He stopped himself. "Except the marriage license fee is up to $35,000. Where would we get that kind of money?"

"And I couldn't leave my family," Rose said. "Especially now. I don't think my mom's health is very good."

He looked at her with concern. "Really?"

I shouldn't have said that! Rose thought. It was dangerous to admit illness. A sick person who couldn't pull their weight in society could be reported to Relevance... But Decker would never say anything, Rose assured herself. He loved her. He'd just admitted that. "My dad says she's just depressed," Rose said with a shrug. "I'm sure it's nothing serious."

Decker pulled her close. "Promise you won't go Pioneer on me," he whispered against her cheek. "Just promise me that much."

"I promise," she said, afraid it was a promise she might not be able to keep.

Chapter 8
VIOLET

The pounding on the door woke them all.

Violet bolted upright. Not a trace of sim sun filtered through the bedroom window. Morning hadn't yet arrived. "Does anyone know what time it is?"

The pounding got louder. She heard her father say, "Hold on, I'm coming!"

Daisy switched on the tiny sudoflicker by her bed mat. "Five a.m.," she said, yawning.

"Maybe it's a patient," Rose said. On occasion a medical emergency would arise and her father would be summoned to the hospital or, more infrequently, to the lab. But that usually came via a phone call...

"**Save The Earth Police**! Open the door!"

Violet said, "Quick, Daisy! Hide Pip!"

"Oh, no!" Daisy gasped. She pushed the dog under the cover and instructed Pip sternly: "Pip, *stay*!" Luckily, Pip wasn't a barker. He was asleep again before she and Rose and Violet had even left the bedroom.

There were four S.T.E.P. officers standing in the living room. "Are you Sunellen Budd?" one asked.

"I am," her mother said calmly. *Good,* Mom, Violet thought; never show them that you're afraid. "How can I help you, officers?"

"We've received a report that you haven't been meeting your recycling quota. When was the last time you deposited your Plastica materials into the building's collection cart, Mrs. Budd?"

Violet saw her father's arm go around her mom's shoulders. He pulled her close to him.

"Recycling? Why—why I thought I recycled just yesterday..."

A shiver went down Violet's spine. Her mother sounded unsure. Daisy, standing beside her in the semi-darkness, took Violet's hand.

"You *thought?*" one of the officers said gruffly. "Don't you know?"

"I'm Dr. Prentiss Budd, officer," her father intervened. "And I would appreciate it if you would lower your voice when you address my wife."

The officer checked the notes on his clipboard. "I know who you are, sir, but this is a serious crime—"

Her father cut him off. "There was no crime committed here, I assure you," he said. "My wife has never missed a Plastica collection. Whoever reported this is mistaken."

The officer shook his head. "I don't think so, sir. It says right here..."

"I don't care what it says," her father insisted. "It's a mistake!"

One of the other officers, a tall, pale man with a sneering expression, nudged the officer standing to his left. "Well, would you look at that," he said, staring at Violet and her two sisters who were watching the scene in frozen silence. "Not one, not two, but *three*! I told you they were Wasters," he said with a snicker.

"What did you say?!" her father bellowed. He took a step toward the man, fists clenched. The other two officers prevented him from moving any farther. "I want your name and certification number! Now!"

"I apologize, Dr. Budd," the first officer said. He turned to glare at the palefaced one, who shrugged.

"Look, if you're sure about this, if the report really was made in error—"

"I'm sure," her father said. "Now please leave these premises! But before you go, I want this idiot's name. Or I'll call Chief Mulligan!"

Violet was pleased to see the paleface flush an angry red. She knew her father had saved the life of S.T.E.P. Chief Mulligan's wife when no other doctor could. Chief Mulligan's wife had begun to show signs of irrelevance—forgetting things, not showing up for work—and her father had refused to refer her to Relevance Lab for research. The Chief owed him more than one favor.

The first officer nodded. "Yes, sir, and I'm sorry about this." He wrote Paleface's name and certification number on a piece of paper and handed it to her father.

"Glacier Starr," her father read. "I'll remember that name."

Daisy's hand grasped Violet's tightly. "Ellis Starr's cousin," she whispered. "She's in Moonrock's class with me."

Violet nodded. She wished the police would leave already. When the officer opened the apartment door, Violet saw that some of their neighbors had already gathered in the hallway. One of them had given the false report about her mother, she thought. But which one? Violet knew they all resented the fact that a family with triplets lived among them. They thought it tarnished the building's reputation.

Well, too bad! Violet thought. *We're here, get used to it!* Except that she wished they *weren't* here. She wished her father would relent and apply for Pioneer dispensation so that they could live free and never endure humiliation like this again.

Chapter 9

PRENTISS

He frowned at the results of the G study in front of him. It was not the tidy, uniform genomic map he'd urgently hoped for. Rather, Sunellen's 3-D holographic head chart showed irregularities in her brain function that were not present at her last checkup six months ago. The changes showed especially in the cerebrum, the part of the brain responsible for memory.

Or, in Sunellen's case, memory *loss*.

He rechecked the results. He knew what it was *not*: Not Alzheimer's, because that disease had been eradicated more than 50 years ago, thanks to the late Dr. Jonas Everett Salk and his discovery of Exprolamine. One of Salk's distant ancestors had discovered a cure for an old paralytic disorder called poldoid or poleon or something like that. It was a disease so ancient he couldn't even remember the name, only that it had killed and maimed millions of humans all over the world.

Sunellen, just like everyone else in the population, had been vaccinated against Alzheimer's and was totally immune to it.

It wasn't cancer, because that, too, had been wiped out with the discovery of Genocell just 15 years ago. Genocell had been developed right here in this very lab. He, himself, had worked on the team along with Carla Brooker, Harlan Cedar, Gustave Rivers and other teams from Clearpoint View and Rainbow Arc Domes. After years of dedicated hard work, their research had finally paid off: Genocell, extracted from desalinated ocean water and Neufab, the chemical the very walls were made of! The answer to medicine's most unyielding puzzle had been in front of them—actually surrounding them—the entire time.

Each team had been awarded the coveted Global Sustainment Prize, the highest honor given by the Board of Presidents. Each member of the team had also been given $10 million dollars and unlimited freedom to travel the InterDome Automotion Highway, no questions asked.

Prentiss sighed. Well, he had a question: What was this new mystery?

He looked up from the G study. Thankfully, the lab was still empty. He'd arrived early, before any of the others were due to show up for work. He must not allow anyone else to see Sunellen's head chart.

He switched off the hologram and stored it in his personal computerized file, making sure it was locked. Then he sat at his desk for several moments, his head in his hands.

The S.T.E.P. report had *not* been a mistake. Sunellen *had* forgotten to recycle. He had suspected as much, but had hoped against hope he was wrong.

"Really, Prentiss, I don't need another test. It hasn't even been a year since the last one!" she'd protested.

"I know, darling, but humor me, okay?" He'd kissed her and told her how much he loved her and she had reluctantly agreed to the test.

So now he knew the truth. The horrible, heartbreaking truth. Sunellen's brain looked like it was aging far more quickly than normal.

And she was not the only one. He had begun to see the same odd pattern in some of his other patients' G studies. He hadn't told a soul—not yet, anyway, but he knew he would have to do something, and soon. Other researchers would discover it in their own patients, and it would become common knowledge, and then Sunellen's fate would be out of his hands.

He stood and began to pace the lab. Its white walls blinked steadily with thousands of tiny computerized lights. Each one of those lights represented someone's destiny, he thought morosely. They contained the biological record of every person in Blue Skies Dome, beginning at the moment of their birth.

Every city in every domed state had a lab like this one. He wondered if the same anomaly was showing up in the other labs or if this was just a Blue Skies problem.

Perhaps he would call Bill Simmons over in Rainbow Arc. He and Bill had gone to medical school together in Vermont. Bill had chosen to remain up north, while he, Prentiss, had opted for California. They'd stayed friends over the years, although they hadn't been in touch for a while.

It would be risky, he knew. Suppose the same thing *were* happening over there? Bill would be compelled to notify his own Relevance Board that Blue Skies was having the same problem.

If this thing—whatever it was—was unique to Blue Skies, if it was a local problem, it might be easier to find the cause. It might have something to do with the environment here. Perhaps a glitch in the Dome mechanism? In the SumbraSteel itself? Prentiss was shocked that he had even formed these thoughts. To suggest that the Dome was a less-than-perfect instrument of life sustenance was treasonous and punishable by years of imprisonment. He was a well-respected doctor and had many connections with powerful people because of his contribution to the discovery of Genocell, but even he was not above a charge of treason!

The door to the lab opened and Drs. Brooker and Cedar walked in.

"Dr. Budd!" Carla Brooker said, giving him a wave. "What's the good word?"

She always greeted him with ancient expressions from history she had read about. He found this one especially meaningless. The good word? There were millions of good words, he thought. *Love. Health. Freedom.*

He chose to ignore the question and smiled. "Good morning, Dr. Brooker. Dr. Cedar."

Harlan Cedar, wearing his usual dour expression, merely nodded.

Prentiss checked his wrist crystal. If he did decide to call Bill Simmons, he would have to wait until lunch break or even until tonight, after work.

He would have to be very careful. And very discreet.

Sunellen's life might depend on it.

Chapter 10

A SAMPLE ESSAY

Recent Ancient History, Mrs. Budd
June 15, 2275

A BEST-CASE SCENARIO FOR PLANET EARTH

By Daisy Budd

Ever since our planet was nearly destroyed by the tragic consequences of Global Warming, theories have been put forth as to how we can restore Earth to its former viability. How do we set about reforesting our millions of acres of depleted land? How do we eliminate the carbon dioxide that has been poisoning the air we used to breathe before the Domes were erected? How do we get the oceans to recede to their former levels before the worldwide tsunamis swept away entire continents?

Perhaps the answers to these questions lie in understanding what happened to cause the devastation in the first place:

1. **Fossil Fuels.** People used them to run their cars and trucks, etc. without regard to the effect it had on our trees and on the air we breathed. The trees absorbed those poisonous emissions until they could no longer do so. When the forests began to decay, they spewed huge amounts of carbon dioxide back into the air, thus warming the planet and melting the arctic ice.

2. **Fracking.** This was a practice designed to extract even **more** fossil fuels from rock! It was done by a system of high-volume hydraulic fracturing. What it did accomplish at the end was the fracturing of a whole way of life for billions of people!

3. **Ignorance.** Scientists tried to warn the human race that the above examples were taking a toll on our planet, but no one would listen. They accused the scientific community of using scare tactics. They did not believe Global

Warming was real until the temperatures began to rise to over 120°F degrees every day, and the worldwide droughts began in earnest.

I believe our Earth can and will revert to its former glory by, One, trusting our scientific community. After all, they know more about our planet than most people. Two, we must abide by the rules of our Dome:

A. Always recycle. Never miss a collection!

B. Ration your use of sudoflickers. Do not waste luminates. Do not waste **anything!**

C. Support our hydrogen fuel workers who are striving to produce the kind of fuel that will not harm our planet. Although that goal hasn't yet been achieved—we must first harness wind power and solar energy to produce the fuel, but this won't be possible until our dome can be safely opened indefinitely—we must support the folks who work in the plants. Go Hydrogen Fuelers!

There are some who say the atmosphere beyond our Dome is already viable. They believe that somewhere, probably in the northern or eastern territories, the oceans have returned to normal levels and that some sea life has reappeared. I have also heard speculation that crops like corn and wheat have begun to grow. This may be true, since fossil fuels have not been poisoning our planet for 150 years. Still, I don't believe we should take chances by opening our Dome until the government—specifically the Board of Presidents—gives the all-clear signal.

Yes, I firmly believe that one day we will be able to breathe real air and eat food that has been planted and grown in real soil. But until that day, we need to be patient and trust our scientists and our government.

Chapter 11

DAISY

She'd lost her best friend. The last time she'd seen Calla Brown was three weeks ago. She'd been trying to call her on her crystal chip ever since, but all she kept getting was a blank screen.

She would never see Calla again. Once people went Pioneer, no one ever heard from them. That was because no messages could penetrate the SumbraSteel dome, which was fine for keeping out the poisons in the atmosphere, but wasn't fine for people who lost their best friend.

Friends were never easy to find for people like her. Being a triplet and a teenager was a double threat. Oh, how she hated being different!

"Stop looking like the world has ended!"

Startled, she looked up to see Violet standing in front of her, frowning. The school corridor was crowded and noisy, as kids rushed from one class to another. It was five o'clock, only one class to go before dismissal.

"I miss Calla," she said with a shrug.

"I know you do," Violet said, her voice holding a tinge of sympathy. "If you'd just try to convince Dad to go Pioneer, there's a good chance you'll see her again!"

"Quit trying to manipulate her!" Rose said, coming up behind Violet. "There's no guarantee she'll see her friend again if we go—" Rose paused, unwilling to even say the word. "Besides, Daisy's fine with staying right here in Blue Skies, aren't you, Daze?"

They were each headed to a different class—Violet to Chemistry, Rose to Advanced Physics and she, Daisy, to Ancient Music, in which they were learning about a style of music called Rock and Roll, from way back in the 20th century.

They had never been permitted to take a class all three together; it would have attracted too much attention, none of it good.

Daisy sighed. She loved her sisters. They were wonderful, decent people, both of them much prettier than she was. Her own blonde hair lacked the silkiness of Violet's black bob or the fire of Rose's glorious red strands. Yes, she loved them but there were times—like now—when she wished she could press a button and make them disappear, like a hologram.

A series of chimes rang out, signaling two minutes to clear the corridor and get to the next class.

"Saved by the chime," Daisy said, edging her way between her sisters. She pasted a smile on her face which never quite reached her eyes.

"See you at home," Rose called after her.

Daisy didn't bother to turn around, hurrying instead to Mr. Jagger's classroom before he closed the door. Mr. Jagger was her favorite teacher. He made what could have been a boring subject come really alive. He understood everything about ancient music; it was even rumored that one of his great, great, great grandparents had been an actual performer of this rock and roll stuff!

Ellis Starr got to the classroom door a nanosec before she did and tried to push it closed before Daisy could enter. When Mr. Jagger appeared behind Ellis to hold the door open, Ellis gave her a taunting sneer. "Waster!" she mouthed silently.

Daisy thought she was used to the insult, but for some reason—maybe because she missed Calla so much—she felt tears come to her eyes. She turned her face away to see Sharkey Collins standing behind her. To her astonishment, he flashed his dimpled grin at her.

She was probably mistaken. He was probably smiling at Ellis. She hurried inside as quickly as she could, sliding into her seat just as Mr. Jagger inserted a song into the HoloDisc box. Music flooded the room. It was a song Mr. Jagger had played to them before called "Satisfaction".

He said it contained the "perfect confluence of rhythm and melody" and that it was a perfect example of the kind of music people used to depend on to make them happy.

Daisy tried to look interested. She made herself move her body in time with the music like some of the other kids were starting to do, but all she could think of was Ellis' silent insult on one hand and Sharkey's gorgeous smile on the other.

She was disgusted with herself. How could she even *like* a boy like Sharkey? He was prejudiced against those who weren't conceived by CPC injections, just like the majority of people were. He thought Yearners, those who wanted to leave the Dome, were traitors. Her mother had once told her that Sharkey suffered from something called poor character development, and that she, Daisy, should have as little to do with people like that as possible. But it had been years since he had called her a Waster. They were only little kids at the time. Couldn't people change? Well, couldn't they?

She sighed. She was kidding herself. Sharkey Collins would never be interested in a triplet. And the way things were in this society, she wasn't sure she could blame him.

Chapter 12

SHARKEY COLLINS

He must be losing his mind. He couldn't believe he had smiled at Daisy Budd earlier today. The freakiest of the freaks in the whole school. In the whole Sector. Maybe even in the whole Dome! But he couldn't help himself. She was so gosh-dome pretty, with her golden hair, almost as blonde as his own. Her eyes were deep blue, the color of that lake—what was it called?—in the state of Nevada. They'd seen holographic slides of it in Moonrock's Pre-Warming geography class last year. Tahoe! That was it! He'd never seen such a deep blue color, except when he looked into Daisy's eyes.

He glanced at the crystal chip on his wrist: Almost 5:30. Ellis was late again. She had asked to meet him after school to discuss plans for the prom, not that he really cared one way or the other. He had asked Ellis to be his date more out of habit than anything else. They'd been a couple since—well, since forever. Or at least that's how it seemed.

"Hey," she said, startling him. "Why so glum, chum?"

He flinched. He hated it when people used those stupid phrases from Medieval English! "You're late," he snapped.

She shrugged. "Jagger made me stay after. That dude creeps me out."

Again those idiotic ancient phrases! Why couldn't she just use regular 23rd-century English? "How come?" he asked, pretending interest.

"Forget it," she said, shrugging. She took his hand and they started walking in the direction of Shady Grove Park.

He had seen the way she'd tried to close the classroom door on Daisy, and he knew Mr. Jagger had seen it as well. Ellis really had it in for Daisy ever since her cousin, Glacier, the S.T.E.P. guy, had been reprimanded for using the W word in front of Daisy's father. Speaking of creeps, Sharkey thought. Glacier Starr was a mean one. They said he once caught a dog who'd escaped to Outside and ripped it apart with his bare hands before he even took it to a Relevance Lab.

They reached the park and chose a bench near the waterfall hologram. It was close to dinnertime, and the park was relatively deserted. The waterfall volume was on high and he could barely hear what Ellis was saying. Something about her gown being pink, so he should buy her a purple New-Bloom corsage. Afterwards they would be going to Sector 12, where one of her friends— he couldn't quite make out who—would be hosting a marathon after-prom party. Blah-blah-blah, to quote one of Ellis' ancient phrases.

If his father ever knew he might be interested in Daisy Budd, the triplet, he'd probably send him to S.T.E.P. Juvey. Or maybe even to a Relevance lab to be tested for insanity where he'd probably be judged irrelevant to society and discarded. Or worse—to be fodder for experiments.

"Are you listening to me, Sharkey Collins?" Ellis demanded, shoving him hard in the ribs with her elbow. "What's the matter with you, anyway? You've been acting weird for weeks, now. Are you getting sick?"

He was sick, all right. Sick of Ellis and her snobby ways. Everyone thought she was so pretty, with her full pink lips and cute, turned-up nose. He'd thought so too, at first. But once he'd gotten to know her—and her darker moods—she no longer seemed so pretty. What was that other old phrase? Never read a book through its cover? Judge a cover from a book? He couldn't quite remember. The point was, you really never know someone until you—well, until you get to know them.

"I'm listening," he said, with a trace of annoyance. "You want a purple corsage. Fine. We're going to Sector 12 after the prom, also fine." He surreptitiously heightened the holographic volume button on his side of their bench. The sound of the waterfall roared up a notch. Ellis was so busy talking she didn't even notice.

He had better get control of himself. Maybe he *was* getting sick. There were rumors of something going around—a virus, maybe—that made people forget things. How else to explain his feelings for a Waster? A harsh word, yes, but true nevertheless. Daisy's mother hadn't gone to CPC for shots in order to have a baby like a normal person. That's why she'd given birth to—he could barely form the word in his mind—*triplets.* He had no doubt that if Daisy's father hadn't been so important and necessary to their Dome, one of the triplets—maybe even two of them—would have been discarded.

And that was another reason Ellis hated Daisy. She felt the Budd family got away with all sorts of infractions just because Dr. Budd was one of those researchers who helped cure cancer. Plus, he had once saved the life of Police Chief Mulligan's wife, Augusta. "I don't care," Ellis had said. "It's just not fair."

Maybe she was right. He looked at Ellis, who was still jabbering away about the prom. He leaned closer and stopped the jabber with a kiss. Which led to another kiss. Which led to a few more.

And all the while he was kissing Ellis, he kept thinking of Daisy. Which was not only unfair, it was downright dangerous.

Chapter 13

ROSE

It was great news. Decker had been granted early acceptance to Government Training School, the most exclusive college under the Domes! Only those students with the highest I.Q.'s and the best records for citizenship were accepted. All four current presidents had graduated with honors from GTS.

It was also terrible news. The school was located in Clearpoint View Dome, way across the country in Wyoming.

"I know what you're thinking," Deck said as they walked toward Wafer Wonderland, the exclusive restaurant in Sector 4, where they would be sharing a celebratory dinner with Decker's parents.

"But we'll crystal call each other every day, and I'll be home for two weeks next summer, and maybe you could come up for a visit sometime before next Domes-Day..."

He was trying to be optimistic, and she was trying not to let him see how her heart was breaking. "I'm so proud of you, Deck," she said, wishing she'd agreed to elope with him when he'd asked her last month. *I'm being selfish*, she thought. This was the opportunity of a lifetime for him. This was Decker's whole future!

"When are you leaving?" she asked, dreading his answer.

He gripped her hand tightly as they crossed Main Street, carefully skirting the hovercycles and battery carts that always clogged the road at this time of day. "In two weeks," he said quietly, a trace of regret in his voice.

Her heart fell. Only two weeks! Even before high school graduation! She knew what would happen once Decker got to college. He would meet beautiful, smart girls who were normal—who weren't a triplet. It was so unfair! Decker would leave and she would be left here in Blue Skies without him. Suddenly the thought of staying or leaving the Dome didn't matter. Without Decker, she didn't care where she lived. Or even *if* she lived, she thought morosely...

"So, Rose, what are your plans for after high school?" Decker's father asked. They were seated in one of the most private areas of the restaurant, where the other diners spoke in hushed tones and the atmosphere was one of polite refinement.

"I'll probably go to T.A.," she replied with a modest shrug. This was the first time she'd met Decker's parents and she found Mr. Bliss slightly intimidating. He kept watching her with an appraising gaze.

"Teachers Academy? Well, I suppose there's nothing wrong with that," he shrugged.

Who said there was anything wrong with it? she thought defensively. "Well, I guess it's not as prestigious as the Government Training School," she said modestly, taking a tiny bite of her salad wafer.

"My dear, very few schools are," Mr. Bliss said with a satisfied grin.

"T.A.'s a *great* school, Dad," Decker said with a trace of irritation. "Rose's mom went there and she's one of the best teachers I've ever had!"

"I'm sure she is, darling," Deck's mother intervened. She smiled and turned to Rose: "I love the color of your hair, dear. Are both your sisters redheads too?"

Her voice carried in the subdued atmosphere of the restaurant, and Rose could sense the shock of the other diners nearby. "Um, no," she said in a tiny voice. "Violet's hair is black. Daisy is blonde. We're fraternal. That means—"

"Yes, we know what that means," Mr. Bliss said sharply. His face had turned deep red. She saw him give Decker a look that said, "See what you'd be letting yourself in for if you stayed with this freak?"

The rest of the meal passed in strained silence. For once, she couldn't wait to leave Decker's side and go home to her family. To her parents, who loved her. To the cause of all her pain.

Chapter 14

VIOLET

RECYCLING REAPS REWARDS!!!

It was the ubiquitous slogan you saw everywhere, every day, under every Domed city in America. Plastered onto walls, as background for holographic newscasts, on tee shirts and battery carts and hovercycle bumpers. Recycling was the most important thing a citizen could do to speed the recovery of the planet since Global Warming had devastated Earth centuries ago.

Another slogan was: **FAILURE TO RECYCLE MAY RESULT IN IMPRISONMENT AND/OR RELEVANCE DETERMINATION!**

Violet hugged herself tightly. That one terrified her. This morning, after her mother had gone to the local Simulated Food Center for groceries, her father had sat the three of them down and told them what had really happened: "There was no mistake in that S.T.E.P. report," he'd said in a voice barely above a whisper because of the thinness of the Neufab walls of their apartment. "Your mother did forget to recycle."

Rose gasped. "Dad, that's impossible! Mom would never—"

"It happened," her father interrupted, pausing. "But there's an explanation. She's not well."

It was Daisy's turn to gasp: "Dad! What's wrong with her?"

"I'm not sure. Yet." Her father began to pace in their tiny living room. "I'm working on it," he said. "I think it may be a virus specific to Blue Skies. I've spoken with Bill Simmons over in Rainbow Arc. He said there were no health problems over there."

"What can we do?" Rose asked. She felt very afraid for her mother. Her incredibly kind and loving mother who had insisted on saving her baby, Rose, when the entire Dome was against letting her stay born.

"I want you to make certain that Mom doesn't miss a recycling pickup again," her father said. "Do I have your word?"

All three of them nodded in unison. Daisy stood and ran to him and gave him a hug. Rose did the same.

Violet, frowning, remained seated. "When you say 'local virus' what do you mean? Does it have something to do with the Dome itself?"

"Violet, that's ridiculous!" Daisy exclaimed. "You know the Dome is perfectly safe for us to—"

"Perfectly safe?" Violet interrupted. "How would you know? How would *anyone* really know what goes on inside Dome Maintenance?"

Rose plopped down onto the sofa, closing her eyes in exasperation. "Oh, no. There she goes again. Dad, tell her she's being ridiculous!"

But her father remained strangely silent, his dark blue eyes piercing in their intensity. Eyes just like Violet's own. "I don't know, honey," he said with a tired sigh. The remark was meant for Daisy but he was looking at Violet.

"You mean such a thing could be possible?" Daisy asked. "I thought nothing harmful could pass through SumbraSteel, not even something as small as a virus!" Just then, Pip wandered into the living room and leapt onto Daisy's lap. She began to massage him between his ears and the little dog closed his eyes in ecstasy.

"Of course it's possible!" Violet said before her father could answer. "It's even probable! Stop being so naive, Daisy!"

"Girls! Please stop bickering." He looked so forlorn. Violet's heart ached. "Will you promise to remind your mother about recycling? And I need all of you to— well—to watch your mom for any other odd behavior. If you see anything out of the ordinary, will you let me know right away?"

"Of course we will, Daddy," Violet said.

He gave her a small smile. "Violet, promise me that you won't share your opinions about Dome Maintenance with anyone. Not even your activist friends."

But she refused to promise. She *couldn't* promise that. Because her "activist" friends, as her father insisted on calling the Truth Be Told group, felt exactly the same way. It had been over 200 years since the last Dome was erected. The effects of the Warming *must* have improved, at least somewhat, since then. But the Board of Presidents and the Dome Maintenance Committee still refused to open the Dome except for a few measly minutes each year on Domes-Day.

She didn't trust the Board of Presidents. Oh, River Robles, who oversaw the Northern cities, might be okay; he actually *lowered* Dome taxes for his territory last month. And Ruby Jewell from East America seemed genuine enough. One of the Hydrogen Fuel Plants there was said to be making real progress because President Jewell was so dedicated to ending Domed existence.

But Lance Stickers from the South and their own Drew Blacker from here in the West were another story. They kept raising Blue Skies taxes every year—by $1500!—because, they said, vandals were always trying to break through the SumbraSteel and repairs were costly.

By "vandals", Violet knew they meant groups like Truth Be Told. More and more people were beginning to suspect what TBT and the other groups were almost certain of: that the Board had good reason to keep the Dome closed because of all the tax money they were getting!

A cynical way of looking at things, perhaps. But also, Violet thought, most likely the truth!

Something had to be done. If it ever became known, the reality of her mother's illness would end in tragedy. It was a fact of life in Blue Skies and, to a lesser extent, in the other Domed cities: Once a human became too ill to work or contribute to the recovery of the planet, they automatically became irrelevant. They would be labeled a Drainer—someone who drained Earth's resources instead of contributing to them. They breathed the simulated air, ate the simulated food, downed the simulated medications, which they could no longer repay.

Drainers were automatically sent to Relevance Labs, where they were subjected to experiments to develop new medications and even, it was whispered, new sources of food. Exactly like the stray animals that were bred and kept in cages by the thousands in the Labs.

To think her own mother might be destined to suffer the same, horrible fate caused Violet, who almost never cried, to break down. Thank Dome it was almost dark and no one noticed. She hurried to the emergency TBT meeting she had called.

Yes, something had to be done, and soon. She would see to it.

Chapter 15
SUNELLEN

Her head was aching again. It wasn't too bad yet, but she knew it would get worse as the day wore on. Prentiss had said not to worry, that he'd get to the bottom of this—whatever it was—before too long. He would find the right combination of chemicals and she'd be good as new.

She wanted to believe him, but she couldn't. She had never felt pain this severe, not even when she'd had her babies!

The thought of her girls made her smile in spite of the ache in her head. They were so beautiful, even as infants. Each had been born with soft tufts of hair—one light yellow, one blue-black, one gorgeous, burnished red. They had reminded her of that picture in her photo archive of a field of flowers from before the Warming had started: yellow daisies, purple violets, red roses. And that is why she had given them flower names. Their last name, Budd, had been a happy coincidence.

No one had ever seen a real flower, of course, but they were said to have been one of Earth's natural wonders because of their beauty and fragrance which were said to be exquisite. Exquisite, like her girls.

She wished they were happier, though. Even now she could hear Rose weeping softly in her bedroom because her boyfriend, Decker Bliss, was away at Government Training School in Clearpoint View Dome, and poor Rose missed him terribly. They crystal-called each other several times a day, and Rose was even planning to visit him in a few weeks...

A sharp pain interrupted her thoughts. She stood up and the room spun. The pain began in her neck and traveled to her left temple. She held onto the Neufab walls, moving slowly to the open window of her bedroom. She took a deep breath of Domed air but it only served to make her more lightheaded.

Could she be dying? If so, she wondered how much time she had left. Would she still be around for the start of the new term in three weeks? Tears came to her eyes. She loved being a teacher, seeing her students mature and grow. Even Sharkey Collins had made progress this year. His term essay on the History of the Doming of the United States had surprised her by its clarity and organization, even if she disagreed with his views.

There was something else about Sharkey that seemed different, but she couldn't put her finger on exactly what. He seemed more respectful when he addressed her now, and he no longer shifted in his seat as though he couldn't wait to leave her class.

She was probably imagining things. People like Sharkey—and his father, her principal, Jeremiah Collins—rarely changed. They remained stuck in their biased view of the world, refusing to open their minds to ideas the slightest bit different from their own.

Outside, it was already beginning to get dark. Sudoflickers were coming on in the windows of the adjacent apartment buildings. So many buildings, all alike, for miles, as far as the eye could see. How she would have loved to leave Blue Skies for the Pioneer area, to see the possibility of a renewed earth, to breathe real air and smell real flowers...

"Mom? Are you all right?" Rose stood in the doorway, concern in her voice.

"I'm fine," Sunellen said, forcing a smile. "Just thinking about what to cook for dinner. Are you hungry, sweetie?"

Rose came to where she was standing and gave her a hug. "A little. Daze and Vi should be here in a few minutes. Dad called earlier to say he'd be late and that we should start dinner without him."

No surprise there, Sunellen thought. Prentiss had been staying late at the lab quite a bit recently, trying to find out what ailed her and how to cure it. If that were the case, he'd better hurry. The pain in her head was quickly becoming unbearable.

"I'll help with dinner, Mom," Rose said. "What about spaghetti wafers with corn paste?"

"Great idea! I'll start, you set the table..."

"No, Mom, let me do it. Please, just rest, okay?"

Sunellen didn't protest. She was realizing something: Lately, she was never left alone in the apartment. One or another of the girls always seemed to be there with her. She knew in a flash that this must be Prentiss' doing.

They were all afraid she'd forget to recycle again. Or that she would commit some other infraction, like revealing her views about Pioneering to people who thought it was treason just to think about leaving Blue Skies!

Embarrassment warmed her face. Her children were ashamed of her!

She couldn't blame them. Thinking about it now, she honestly couldn't remember if she'd recycled today! Or was it yesterday...? Defeated, she sat back down on her bed. "Thank you, Rose," she said wearily. "I am feeling a bit weak."

Why was this happening? Since Prentiss, bless him, had helped to find the cure for cancer, the average life span in 2275 was 120 years. She wasn't even 55 yet. What had she done to deserve this? She had always tried to be a good person, to do her part for Earth's Recovery. She donated generously to the Hydrogen Refuelers Movement, which was striving to develop a working fuel plant. And she and Prentiss always paid their constantly escalating Dome taxes without complaint.

Yet now she was in real danger of becoming a Drainer. She'd be taken to a Relevance Lab and be experimented on. But why? What was wrong with her?

She didn't have an answer. She suspected no one did.

Chapter 16

DAISY AND ROSE

The beach was crowded, mostly with kids taking advantage of the last day of summer vacation. Three weeks had passed in a flash for Daisy and gone agonizingly slowly for Rose, who was even now checking her watch crystal for a missed call from Decker Bliss.

"I haven't heard from him since yesterday morning," she said miserably. "Do you think he's met someone else?"

"He's probably just neck-deep in schoolwork," Daisy said, exasperated. "He'll call you soon, I promise."

Rose smiled. "Really? Is that the Knowing talking? Or are you just saying that to make me feel better?"

It was the Knowing, but not the good kind. Decker would be calling her soon, but not to say what Rose wanted to hear. "Come on, let's go for a swim," Daisy said, changing the subject. They walked to the water's edge and watched the waves in silence for a while.

Ocean water was the one natural resource Earth had managed to retain in abundance since the Warming, although it was too much of a good thing for some coastal areas: Venice, Italy; New York City; Shanghai, China; Tokyo, Japan; and islands and archipelagos all over the world were obliterated over 100 years ago, during the mega floods of 2168.

Other states, like their own California and, it was said, some of the eastern coastal states like Massachusetts and Connecticut, had escaped relatively unscathed. Luckily, desalination efforts had begun early enough to prevent millions more from dying of thirst. What was that ancient saying? "Water, water everywhere, and not a drop to drink?" Daisy shuddered.

The simulated sun was warmer here at the beach than anywhere else in Blue Skies Dome, and the water felt good as the sisters dove headlong into a wave. They swam for a while and then Rose said she wanted to go back to their blanket to see if Decker had called.

Daisy would not tell her what the Knowing foretold: That Rose and Decker's relationship was doomed. She didn't know when the breakup would occur exactly, or even why, but come it would. The sympathy she felt for her sister was intense.

The Knowing was telling her something else as well: Something bad—really bad—was going to happen to Violet. And soon. Oh, it was so infuriating to have foreknowledge without specifics!

She followed Rose to their blanket, wishing for the zillionth time that she could get rid of this affliction—this curse!

Rose smeared ProTec onto her sister's back. ProTec was supposed to filter out the harmful rays of the sun, but since SumbraSteel prevented any *real* sun from penetrating their dome, it was just a pretense. The Board of Presidents and the politicians insisted on preserving the illusion that the Domed population was living in a natural world instead of a simulated one. Everyone went along with it, probably out of habit. Or because there was no alternative. *Or was there?*

I'm starting to sound like Violet! Rose thought. "Daisy, do you think Pioneer living is possible?"

"What?" Daisy exclaimed, surprised. "What did you say?"

Rose hadn't meant to speak the thought out loud. She shrugged. "It's just that Violet and Mom are so convinced that there's been good recovery Outside. I was just wondering if it's possible."

Daisy knew Rose wouldn't be talking about Pioneering if Decker Bliss were still here.

"I don't know," Daisy said thoughtfully. "No one does. The atmosphere might still be polluted Outside and the Pioneers die the minute they leave the Domes." She thought of her friend, Calla. She missed her so much. Had she survived? Had her parents and her dog, Digger? She would never know, unless her family decided to go Pioneer. And even then there was no guarantee that she'd ever see Calla again. She sighed. The whole idea was unlikely anyway, because of her father's promise to stay in Blue Skies forever as his penance for letting Rose stay born. Penance meant atoning for doing something wrong. Certainly, allowing Rose to stay in the world was not wrong...

Was remaining in Blue Skies a punishment? It certainly wasn't easy living if you were a triplet. Or if you got sick...

As if reading her thoughts, Rose said, "Mom seems better, don't you think?"

It was true. Their mother did seem to be improving. Her headaches were becoming less frequent; more and more she seemed like her old self, and she was eager to be going back to work tomorrow, the first day of school after summer vacation.

Their father, however, still stayed late at work most nights to try to determine what had caused their mother's illness in the first place. "If we don't know what we're dealing with, we won't know how to treat it if the symptoms return," he'd told the three of them recently. "But I don't think it's necessary for you to continue to monitor your mother's behavior any longer. Looks like she's recovering on her own."

Their tiny area of the beach, restricted to multiples (twins) and others who had been born without the help of CDC chemicals, had begun to thin out and sudoflickers were coming on. It was still really warm, though, Rose realized. Uncomfortably so, in fact. Which was unusual. The Dome Maintenance Committee never allowed the population to feel uncomfortably hot in summer or uncomfortably cold in winter. Everything was precision controlled for the utmost safety and satisfaction of the population. Or, at least, that was their slogan: "Everything Just Right, Day and Night!"

Daisy and Rose gathered their blanket, hats and towels and started for home. On their way they passed the main entrance to the beach—the part where the regular kids went.

In the distance, Daisy spotted Sharkey Collins leaning against the lifeguard tower, talking to Ellis Starr. His tanned, Pro-Tec-smeared body glistened in the fading sim sun.

He was by far the most beautiful sight she'd seen all day.

Chapter 17
VIOLET

"So it's agreed. Tomorrow night. Anyone not with us is against us, understand? If anyone is having second thoughts, this would be the time to speak up."

The members of TBT were gathered in their headquarters, the basement of a building in Sector 9. They were all here: Bloo, Clinker, Palmer Davis, and the others. And Brink, of course. He was sitting next to her on the fake earth floor, their arms touching. Twelve brave people who had had enough of Domed existence and were willing to take a chance on improving life for themselves and the rest of the population.

"We all wear black, right?" Clinker asked.

"From head to toe," Violet said. They couldn't risk being seen anywhere near the Dome Maintenance office, especially since the S.T.E.P. penalty for trespassing anywhere near it would be a $5000 fine and five points on their record.

Violet couldn't afford another point on her record, let alone five. She was already up to 49 points, once for getting caught trying to save a cat that had escaped a Relevance Lab. The poor creature had had an eye removed and was howling in pain, and she'd picked it up instinctively, intending to bring it home where Daisy, her animal-loving sister, would know what to do. A lab technician had come running out of the lab, pulled the cat from her arms, and reported Violet to S.T.E.P. That infraction had put 28 points on her record. A few weeks ago, a neighbor reported her for making an "unpatriotic diatribe" against the Dome. She'd been arguing with her sister, Rose—*in their own apartment*!—about how brave it would be to go Pioneer and taste real freedom for the first time. Because Neufab walls were so thin, she'd been overheard. Twenty-one more points! Plus, she'd had to spend a sleepless night in S.T.E.P. Juvey and she didn't want to see that place again. Not ever.

"I'll bring the blueprints," Palmer Davis said. "And the formula for the Dome locks," he added. Palmer was a quiet boy, rail thin, with artificial lenses he kept losing. They'd tried to correct his vision the usual way—by injecting his corneas with OcReJuv, which should have solved the problem in seconds—but something in his genetic makeup had rejected the medication.

To look at him no one would ever guess that Palmer was so brave; brave enough to risk life imprisonment for trying to break open Blue Skies Dome in the name of freedom. His father, a chemist who had once worked with the Dome Maintenance Committee, had been caught planning the same thing five years ago and was now in jail forever.

"Thanks, Palmer," Brink said, and there was a general murmur of appreciation from the others.

Violet smiled at Brink. She was glad to see him enthusiastic again. For a while there, he'd expressed doubts about their mission. She'd assumed he was being pressured at home. Brink's mother, Tawny Trayor, was an aide to President Drew Blacker, who served (ruled) Western America, which included Blue Skies. His father, Harden Trayor, was a member of the CPC, the Commission on Population Control. Determined Domers, both of them. Which was why she was so surprised when Brink had stopped her in the school corridor about a year ago and whispered that he'd heard about her rebel group and he wanted in.

Naturally, she pretended to know nothing about any rebel group, but he was persistent. Plus, he was one of the best-looking boys in the whole school. Not beautiful-handsome like that creep Sharkey Collins. Ruggedly handsome like—well, like *sexy*, with black wavy hair almost as dark as hers. His green eyes seemed to seek the truth in everything. She was instantly smitten.

He'd proven himself to be an asset to Truth Be Told, working late compiling flyers, tactfully recruiting new members and keeping their existence totally under the radar.

He planned to apply to medical college after graduation next month, much to his parents' dismay. They had him slated for GTS, the same Government Training School her sister, Rose's boyfriend, Decker Bliss, attended. The fact that Brink wanted to be a doctor, like Violet's father, made her love him even more.

She and Brink had even talked about getting married someday, after both of them were out of college and settled in a career. By that time, hopefully all the Domes would be opened and they would be breathing free air.

But first things first.

They would meet precisely at midnight tomorrow night. Four of them would stand guard outside the Maintenance building with their sensitivity earpins turned up high in order to capture any sound.

Four others, including Clinker, would scale the building's facade to the roof, which led, after half a mile of maze-like turns, to the open/close mechanism of the Dome. They would radio the rest of the group the moment they reached their destination.

The last group was comprised of Violet, Brink, Bloo and Palmer Davis. It would be their job to actually open the Dome, using the formula Palmer's father had bequeathed him. With the demagnetizer Brink had in his possession, they would dismantle the lock springs according to the very complicated, and very secret, formula.

It was to Palmer's credit that he had guarded that formula with his life, especially when the S.T.E.P. had broken into his apartment after his father's imprisonment.

They'd searched every inch of the place for the dome-locking formula—looking everywhere except Palmer's eye lens case, which was hiding in plain sight in the middle of his bed.

"To Freedom!" Violet said, raising her hands, fists clenched, above her head.

"To Freedom!" the others chorused.

To beautiful, beautiful freedom, Violet thought, tears coming to her eyes. Then, Brink's hand in hers, she followed the others into the dark, soundless night.

Chapter 18
PRENTISS

He was beginning to detect a pattern. Sunellen had been recovering nicely from what he had begun to call the "unsettled virus". Her memory had improved (she'd remembered on her own to fill the recycle cart for the last two collections) and her headaches had nearly subsided. But then, last night, on the eve of her return to teaching, she'd wakened with a throbbing pain in her left temple. He'd administered a shot of painkiller and she'd gone back to sleep. But this morning she appeared pale and disoriented.

"Stay home today," he'd begged. "Give yourself another day to rest."

She'd refused, as he'd known she would. "I'm fine," she'd insisted, although she clearly wasn't. "The first day of school is so important, you know that, Prentiss!"

He knew that. A teacher who did not show up for the first day of class would incur a lot of questions. Questions like, Was Sunellen Budd so sick that she had to miss the first day? Sick enough to never teach again?

Was this a Relevance problem? Had she become a Drainer? Someone who took from society but did not give back?

Prentiss studied his notes. It was a cycle: The headaches would worsen at night, then Sunellen would get pale and even have slight tremors for several days, then slowly she would start to feel better.

Other patients had shown similar symptoms, namely Augusta Mulligan, the wife of the Chief of Police Cliff Mulligan. That had been several months ago. Then, last week, she'd crystal-called him and asked if he wouldn't mind coming to their apartment, over in Sector 10. It was quite a distance away, but you did not refuse a request from the wife of the Chief of Police.

So he'd gone to their apartment to find the Chief himself in bed, pale as NeuFab, complaining of headaches.

"It woke me up last night," the Chief said. "I've never had pain this bad. What is it, Prentiss?"

Prentiss shook his head. "I'm not sure," he admitted. "But I'm beginning to see more and more of it."

The Mulligans looked surprised. "Oh, my," Augusta said. "Is it some sort of new plague, do you think?"

The word hung in the air. A *plague*? He hoped it wasn't that. "No, of course not. It might just be some sort of virus. We'll get to the bottom of it soon."

"A virus? But how could that be? Doesn't SumbraSteel filter out..." Before the Chief could finish, Prentiss gave him a shot of painkiller, told him to rest for another day, and turned to leave.

"Wait," the Chief said, and calling him back. "No need to report this to Relevance, right?" he whispered. Prentiss could see the fear in the Chief's eyes.

"No, of course not," Prentiss said, reassuringly, and made himself smile with an assurance he did not feel.

He could get into serious trouble by failing to report this virus, or whatever it was, to Relevance. He frowned as he sat at his desk in the empty lab. How he hated to report anyone! It was barbaric, what went on in those labs. He didn't know how the Relevance Laws had become so strict, but they were entrenched in every city under a Dome and no one ever questioned them.

Just yesterday, Harlan Cedars had told him of an "incipient epidemic" he was finding among his patients. "People forget things. Bad headaches." Harlan had looked at him with his usual scowl. "You encountering anything like that, Budd?"

Prentiss pretended surprise. "No, Harlan. At least, not yet."

He listened as Harlan called a Relevance Lab and gave them the names of his patients who had been afflicted. Those poor people, he'd thought. Please let me find a cure before I'm compelled to do the same.

He looked down at his notes: *Headaches worse at night. Symptoms, including memory loss and tremors, seem to improve in one sector before showing up in another. Duration of symptoms vary from one to two weeks.*

What would make people lose their memory? What could cause terrible head pain? What was not contagious but kept popping up in sectors miles apart?

He sensed he was honing in on the answer. Maybe not a virus. Perhaps something else. Something airborne? Something *atmospheric*?

He bolted upright in his chair. Something in the Dome's atmosphere? Oxygen! The lack of oxygen affected memory! Oxygen deprivation resulted in brain damage. His patients weren't exactly brain damaged, but what if they were slowly, *very* slowly, being deprived of just a tiny bit of oxygen? And not continuously, but sporadically? A tiny bit of oxygen loss every other week or so...?

It couldn't be! Prentiss thought. Something wrong with the Dome's mechanism? The thought itself was treasonous!

But it had taken hold of him, and he couldn't let it go.

Chapter 19

DAISY

She'd hardly slept at all last night. First, the Knowing had tortured her with unspecific warnings about Violet. Then she'd had nightmares about Pip escaping to Outside and being brought to a Relevance lab for experimentation. She didn't know which was worse. As they were getting ready to leave for school this morning, Daisy had taken Violet aside: "Don't do whatever it is you're planning to do!" she'd whispered.

Violet pretended not to know what she meant. "I'm planning to get to school on time," she said, "so let's do that, okay?"

"Violet! I mean it! Something very bad is going to happen if you go through with—" she paused. "—with whatever crazy thing you're thinking of doing!"

When she saw Violet's complexion redden slightly, she knew the Knowing was right.

"Hey!" Rose called from the doorway to their apartment. "It's getting late! What are you two whispering about?"

"Nothing!" Daisy and Violet chorused at the same time.

"In other words, something you don't want me to know about. Does it have to do with Decker?"

"Crackling Neufab!" Violet exclaimed with annoyance. Not everything is about you or your Domer boyfriend!"

"He is not a Domer!" Rose protested. "And I'm not even sure he's my boyfriend anymore since I haven't heard from him in almost a week and he won't return my crystal—"

"Enough!" Violet said, holding her hands against her ears. She glared at Daisy. "See what you've started?"

Defeated, Daisy knew that nothing she could say would prevent Violet from going ahead with whatever crazy stunt she was planning. They walked to school in virtual silence, each absorbed in her own unhappy thoughts.

Schools in all the Domed states remained open year round with a few breaks in between. Classes were held in three-month sessions with two weeks vacation after each session: September through November; December through February; March through May; and June through August.

This September session would be the last for all of them. At the end of November, Rose would be off to Teachers Academy; Violet to Laws Dominion over in Rainbow Arc, where she would study for her Dome Law degree. "When I earn my degree, I hope to help humanity break the shackles of repression and bring some fresh new laws into the legislative Dome!"

Rose had actually written that in an essay last year for her History of Regulations class and old Mrs. Crumblebrick had been horrified. She'd sent her mother a note: "Sunellen—Please have a talk with your daughter about her political statements which, in my opinion, are inappropriate and inflammatory. Sincerely, Louisa Crumblebrick." She'd attached the essay to the note and slipped it beneath her mother's classroom door.

Violet and her mom had giggled about it at home that night, but her father wasn't pleased: "She's right, Violet. You have to be careful about what you say and to whom you say it. Not everyone shares your opinion about Domed society."

"*Doomed* society you mean!" Violet snapped. "Wasn't there a time in this country when people could speak their mind about pretty much anything and not feel threatened?"

"You're talking about pre-Warming society, Vi," her father had replied. "A worldwide catastrophe can change how people view things. Try to be less outspoken—for all our benefit," he'd told Violet.

Not that she'd taken his advice, Daisy sighed now. It was a never-ending argument between Violet and their dad, and to a lesser extent, between Violet and Rose. Their apartment would be much quieter after Vi left for Laws Dominion in Rainbow Arc...

Daisy knew what she would *like* to do after graduating from high school: Storm the Relevance Labs and free all the suffering animals who were undergoing experiments. Why were experiments being conducted in the first place? she wondered. Cures had been found for all the major diseases—she felt a rush of pride thinking of her

Dad and his team's cancer breakthrough—so torturing animals made no sense, right? There was a horrible rumor that the labs were using animals (and even people!) for food. The thought made her physically ill.

In ancient times, there were doctors who actually tried to preserve animal life. They were called veterinarians. She wished with all her heart that she could become a veterinarian! But of course, that profession was illegal in 2275...

If she couldn't rescue animals from the labs, she would get a job at a Simulated Food Center and try to make simulated food taste better. She'd already applied to a Center right here in Blue Skies. When they checked her school records they'd see that she'd taken Advanced Chemistry every year of high school and gotten all A's, and she would surely be accepted. The best thing about going to school right here in Blue Skies was that she'd be able to stay close to Pip, whom she loved with all her heart. She was deep in thought as she walked along the school corridor to her class in Ancient Literature when she bumped into another student.

"Whoa!"

"Oh, sor—" She looked up. It was Sharkey Collins, looking handsomer than ever. She felt herself blush.

"Where're you off to in such a hurry?" he asked, grinning.

"Oh—I—uh—" she stammered. She looked down and saw that she'd dropped her class schedule. She and Sharkey bent to retrieve it at the same time, their heads colliding.

"Ow!" they exclaimed in unison.

"Let me guess," Sharkey said. "Advanced Chemistry?"

"Nope," she said. "Literature. Ancient. I mean, Ancient Literature."

"Hey, me, too," he said. "Don't look so surprised. I *do* read, you know. Holobooks and even PageOgrams."

But she *was* surprised. Surprised that he was talking to her, right here, in public, where everyone could see him talking to a triplet!

Kids glanced their way as they passed by, but no one said anything. Not even Ellis Starr, who thought she'd discovered the reason Sharkey Collins had just broken up with her.

Chapter 20

ELLIS STARR

She was so angry she could hardly speak. When Mrs. Budd asked her a question she stammered, "I—I—could you please repeat that?"

The class snickered. "I asked you to name the year the United States Dome Construction Project was completed—Miss Starr? Please stand!"

Ellis stood up on knees that felt as shaky as a pudding wafer.

"The Dome Project was completed in—in—"

"2103!" Someone said behind her. It sounded like that idiot Clinker James.

"That's correct, Mr. James," said Mrs. Budd, "but I didn't ask you." She turned her gaze back to Ellis. "Not a great way to start the new term, Miss Starr. Please sit down and keep your mind focused."

Ellis hated Ancient Modern History! Who cared when the Domes were completed! Mrs. Budd was such a witch! A Waster witch! Wasters shouldn't be allowed to teach in regular schools with normal kids. They should only be allowed to teach freaky misfits like her Waster triplets! How she hated them! How she hated Daisy Budd!

She had been stunned when Sharkey told her he didn't want to go out with her anymore. They'd had such a great time at the prom. Sharkey had bought her a beautiful purple NewBloom corsage that went beautifully with her pink PlasFabric prom gown. Then they'd gone to her friend Tula Osage's party up in Sector 12. Everything had been going wonderfully until Sharkey brought her home. She'd asked him in for a cake wafer and he refused. He said he had to tell her something and he'd been trying all night to think of a way to say it without hurting her feelings.

Her heart started to beat really hard in her chest. "Sharkey? What is it?"

"We can't see each other anymore, Ellis. I'm sorry. But that's just how it is."

She'd slapped him hard enough to leave her handprint on his cheek. He looked as if he'd expected that. "Hey, I'm really sorry, Ellis, but I'm interested in someone else..." She slapped him again. This time he didn't say a word. He just turned and walked away, leaving her standing alone at the door to her building.

She had to admit that she wasn't all that surprised. He'd been behaving strangely the last couple of weeks, tuning her out while she talked to him, acting preoccupied, or even, well, *bored*. She assumed he was worried about what he'd do after high school. He wasn't smart enough to get into a good school like GTS. She, herself, had been accepted into the S.T.E.P. training program. She had always admired her cousin, Glacier, and dreamed of following in his footsteps. He looked so handsome in his blue S.T.E.P. uniform!

Sharkey's father, Principal Collins, had his heart set on Sharkey going to Teachers Academy, which was laughable. Sharkey Collins—a teacher? It was ridiculous. He hated school even more than she did! He was lazy and not serious about anything. Come to think of it, what did she ever see in him?

He was gorgeous, of course. And goofy in such a cute way. And he was a fabulous kisser...

Her fury returned full blast. Mrs. Budd was still droning on about the Dome Construction Project, how hard it had been to develop the best metal to filter out the pollution, how expensive the Domes were to maintain. Blah-blah-blah, as they used to say in ancient times.

For a while Ellis worried the breakup was her fault. Had she insulted Sharkey somehow? She would call him dopey or lazy occasionally, but she'd just been teasing. Didn't he know that?

When Sharkey told her he was interested in someone else, she'd tried to figure out who it might be. Glory Rockner from Easy Chemistry?

Glory was pretty but she was practically engaged to Art Cloud, the guy from Jagger's music class. (She hated Mr. Jagger! He was such a Waster-lover!) There was Venus Green, from last year's Modern Lit class. Venus had always had a thing for Sharkey, but after she'd been sent to S.T.E.P. Juvey a second time (after she tried to rescue a rabbit from a Relevance Lab) no one had seen or heard from her again.

But Daisy Budd? The triplet? Had Sharkey lost his mind?

She would get even. She didn't know how or when, but she would get even with Daisy Budd for stealing Sharkey Collins away from her.

It was rumored that the Budd family had a dog. And while it wasn't exactly illegal to own a dog as long as it was never allowed Outside, it wasn't really acceptable, either. A dog didn't contribute anything to society. It ate food, it breathed simulated air. It littered the atmosphere with its bodily waste. A dog (or any animal, for that matter) was nothing but a Drainer!

She had asked her cousin Glacier if he'd seen a dog that time he'd been inside the Budd apartment after Mrs. Budd missed a recycling collection. (The very same Mrs. Budd who was at this moment boring everyone with talk about the Dome project!)

"I didn't. But I think I smelled one," Glacier had said.

Well, if she ever had occasion to visit the Budd apartment after she became a S.T.E.P. officer, she would search every inch of the place and if there was a dog there, she would find it.

Yes, she would get even with Daisy Budd. Any way she could. The sooner the better.

Chapter 21

VIOLET

They were lucky. The night seemed unusually dark, the weak light of the sudoflickers barely penetrating the dimness. Most everyone was waiting at the Dome Maintenance gate when she arrived. Everyone except Brink. Violet checked her wrist crystal but just as she was about to call him, he ran up behind her.

"Sorry," he said, out of breath. "My parents didn't get home until late; I had to make sure they were asleep before I left. I ran all the way."

Violet said, "Are you sure they didn't hear you leave?"

"Positive," Brink said, giving her a quick kiss on the cheek. "Now, let's do this thing."

They synchronized wrist crystals. "Midnight. On the dot," Bloo said.

"Palmer? The lock formula? Blueprints?"

"Got 'em."

"Brink? The demagnetizer?"

"Right here," Brink said, holding up an oval-shaped tool that fit into the palm of his hand but that held the power to demagnetize any metal in the known world.

To those who would be standing guard at the entrance, Violet said: "Turn up your sensitivity earpins. And if you hear anything, anything at all, crystal-call us right away. Understood?"

"Yes," they said in unison.

"Clinker? Are you ready?"

He nodded. Clink and the others in his group had their magno-cleats on, shoes that would grab onto the building's facade. It was a long way to the roof, but they'd been practicing their climbing exercises for months and Violet knew—hoped—they were in shape. Once they reached the roof, Clinker would radio down to them and release the climbing coils so that Violet, Brink, Bloo and Palmer could ascend to the roof, and from there to the Dome's open/close mechanism.

They had calculated that the entire mission would take no more than an hour, and that included the actual opening of the Dome. Afterwards, each would run for the safety of home as if their lives depended on it. Which they did.

They watched silently as Clinker and the others climbed the facade and faded into the darkness. Twenty minutes later Violet's wrist crystal pinged softly twice. That was the signal. "They're in!" she whispered triumphantly. Seconds later, the climbing coils slid down.

"You go first," Brink said, handing the demagnetizer to Violet. It was heavier than it looked, and she nearly dropped it. "Careful!" Brink cautioned. "Why don't you tuck it into your boot," he said, which was a good suggestion and she did so. "Bloo, Palmer, you go next. I'll bring up the rear."

Violet gave him a parting kiss. "Love you," she said, as she grabbed onto the coil and began to hoist herself up.

"Love you back," Brink said. "Now go!"

The climb was easier than she thought. After a mere ten minutes, she and the others reached the roof and began to follow along the narrow, maze-like turns which would lead to the Dome mechanism. "Everyone all right?" Violet whispered as they made their way to the tiny speck of light in the distance which was Clinker's pocket sudoflicker. "We're almost there. We can turn our 'flickers on now..."

"Oh, cracklin' NeuFab!" Palmer exclaimed, forgetting to whisper. "Dropped one of my lenses..."

"Shhh—" Violet began. She was interrupted by a sudden, blaring alarm that made her jump and nearly fall. They were enveloped in a piercing torrent of light, a light that nearly blinded them.

"STOP WHERE YOU ARE! PUT YOUR HANDS ABOVE YOUR HEADS! DO NOT MOVE!"

The voice seemed to be coming from everywhere. Violet's first thought: *Palmer's forgetting to whisper must have activated an alarm!* But in another instant she knew that couldn't be right. Because now she could see Clinker and his group coming toward them from up ahead, followed by what looked like an entire S.T.E.P. regiment, guns pointed. Violet and Palmer and Bloo hadn't even reached Clinker's group, so how—?

She turned to see more S.T.E.P. officers approaching from the opposite direction. They were surrounded!

"Brink—" Violet began. She looked at Palmer, pale as a wafer, still on his knees, the dropped lens glinting in the palm of his hand. Bloo stood beside her, visibly trembling. But Brink—Brink was nowhere to be seen. "Brink?" she called again. "Where are you...?" But the ugly answer was already forming in her head.

"On your feet!" A S.T.E.P. officer yelled, poking at Palmer with his rifle. He seemed to know exactly which of Palmer's pockets held the lock formula and the Dome blueprint.

Another officer went straight to Violet. She saw with dismay that it was Glacier Starr. He wore an expression of pure evil.

"The demagnetizer's in her left boot!" said a voice from behind him. And there stood Brink, wearing a grin that broke her heart.

They descended the coils slowly—police in front and behind, with more police waiting below, on the ground.

The four TBTers who had been standing guard were nowhere to be seen. Hopefully they'd had time to get away.

Bloo was sobbing. "How did this happen?"

But the expression on Brink's face said it all. "You didn't really think I'd let you Dome-haters put the lives of millions in jeopardy, did you? You'll get what you deserve now," he said.

"So it was all a lie?" Violet asked her throat aching. "*All* of it?"

He had the decency to blush. She didn't know which was worse: The harsh punishment—life imprisonment or even death—that lay ahead, or the fact that Brink had never really loved her, that he had joined TBT for one purpose only: to betray them.

It was more than she could bear. Like Bloo, and in spite of her determination not to do so, she began to cry.

Chapter 22

ROSE

Decker was kissing her. "Rosebud, I love you so much!" he said, and then he kissed her again. "Will you marry me?"

"Yes!" she exclaimed. "Let's elope today!"

The wail of the sirens jolted her awake. *Just a dream!* Disappointment flooded her. She touched her lips where seconds ago she'd imagined Deck had kissed her.

The sirens were insistent and loud enough to cause Pip to yowl in pain from his place under Daisy's blanket.

"Pip, be quiet!" she heard her sister caution him. Daisy switched her sudoflicker on and peered at Rose. "What's happening?"

"I was dreaming of Decker and—"

"No," Daisy interrupted. "Not your dream! Why are the sirens on?"

"How should I know?" she said crankily. *The dream was so vivid!* She kicked off her blanket and went to the window. It was still dark, and sudoflickers were coming on in the windows of the surrounding buildings. Her crystal watch read 2:00 a.m. Turning from the window, she checked Violet's bed mat. Empty.

"Where's Violet?" she asked Daisy.

Daisy sat up and gasped. "Oh, no. Please, please, no—"

"Daisy? What is it? What's wr—"

"Girls!" Her father's silhouette filled the doorway of their bedroom. "Get dressed. Now!"

"Dad? What's going on?" Rose asked.

"It's Violet," he said. "She's in trouble."

Rose's heart thudded in her chest. "Dad! What happened? Where is Violet?"

"Get dressed and I'll explain," her father said sharply.

In the living room, her parents clung silently to each other as they watched the holographic news:

"Several hours ago, a group of rebels were captured as they attempted to sabotage the mechanism of Blue Skies Dome. Thankfully, the perpetrators were caught before they could inflict any serious damage..." The news anchor shuffled her notes and looked steadily into the camera:

"Normally the names of juvenile offenders are not made public, but due to the seriousness of this crime, we have decided to reveal their identities. They are: Clinker James, Palmer Davis, Bloo Sycamore and Violet Budd, all members of a rebel group called Truth Be Told."

At the mention of Violet's name, her mother burst into tears. "Oh, no! Violet! What have you done?!" she wailed.

"I warned her!" Daisy exclaimed. "I told her not to do it!"

Her father glared at her in anger. "What?! You knew your sister was going to get into trouble and you didn't bother to tell us?"

"I didn't *know*, exactly," Daisy hesitated. "I mean I knew—from the Knowing—that something bad would happen—I tried to stop her, Dad, I really did—" Tears clogged her throat and she sat down heavily on the sofa next to them, her face in her hands.

"It is said that Miss Budd was the ringleader of the group," the news anchor continued. *"She is the daughter of Dr. Prentiss Budd, the noted physician who helped*

develop Genocell, the cure for cancer. We will keep you updated on this story as new details come in."

Her father switched off the hologram and began to pace the floor. "You influenced her!" he said harshly to her mother. "You kept filling her head with those stories about how things used to be before the Warming, feeding her dissatisfaction..."

"I just wanted her to be aware..."

"Aware?!" he repeated. "Are you aware of what could happen to her now? To all of us?"

Rose sat down next to Daisy on the sofa. Just then, Pip wandered into the room, tail wagging. He jumped into Daisy's arms and nestled there.

He's so innocent, Rose thought wistfully; *he has no idea of the trouble we're in.*

"What are we going to do?" Rose asked aloud to no one in particular.

"I've already called the Law Board," her father said wearily. "Someone will be picking me up in a few minutes. We'll go down to the precinct. I'll try to get them to release Violet into my custody." Rose thought he didn't sound at all hopeful about this possibility. He turned to her mother, who appeared pale and shrunken as she dabbed at her eyes with a tis-tab. "Sunellen, forgive me. I didn't mean what I said before. I'm sorry, honey, I'm really sorry." He put his arms around her. "We'll work this out. I promise."

Rose's watch crystal pinged.

"Rose! Maybe you shouldn't answer that," her father warned. "Word spreads fast around here, and a lot of people won't be pleased..."

But it was Decker's face that appeared in the crystal. "It's Deck!" she said excitedly, jumping to her feet and hurrying to the bedroom for privacy.

"Decker? I'm so glad it's you! Did you hear—?"

"I heard," he said. He sounded aloof. Distant. "Rose, listen," he said, speaking quickly. "I'm calling because I—I don't think we should talk to each other anymore. I mean, I think it would be better if you didn't try to contact me."

She stood frozen in the dim sudoflicker light of the bedroom. What was he saying? How many times had he told her he loved her? That he wanted to marry her! "I don't understand—" she began.

"Look. My parents were never happy about our relationship—"

His *parents*? "But you never said anything about—"

"I know," he interrupted. "I didn't want to hurt your feelings. But they have high ambitions for me, Rose. That's why I'm here, at GTS. I might be on the Board of Presidents someday..."

"And you can't risk your reputation by being involved with a triplet, is that it?" Her voice sounded cold and robotic. Exactly how she was feeling.

"No!" Decker insisted. "The triplet thing never mattered to me!" He paused and took a breath. "But this latest business with your sister—I mean, seriously, Rose, breaking into the Dome? What was she thinking? Look, my dad just called me. He said that if I continued to see you, he'd stop paying my tuition. I might be discarded by the family! I might—"

She hung up before he could finish. Sobbing, she lay down on her bed mat and curled herself into a fetal position.

Maybe *this* was the dream, she told herself, and any minute now she would wake to find her sisters, *both* of them, asleep on their bed mats. Wake to find that she still had a boyfriend who loved her and wanted to marry her.

Wake to find that everything was back to normal, that their lives were not changed forever because of Violet's crazy—and *selfish!*—scheme to open the Dome!

But when she thought of Violet—how she must be feeling right now, at this very moment, how frightened she must be—she knew that she, Rose, was the selfish one.

Compared to what was probably in store for Violet, her heartbreak over Decker Bliss was nothing. Nothing at all.

Chapter 23
PRENTISS

He had never felt more helpless in his life. No matter how hard he'd pleaded, the S.T.E.P. people refused to release Violet into his custody, even though he'd sworn to keep her at home under his and his wife's supervision until the case came to trial.

"This was a premeditated crime," the detective in charge told him with stone-faced gravity. "There's no way under the Dome that I can release her. Your daughter will have to stay in Juvenile Detention just like the other criminals."

He winced at the word, *criminals*. Violet was an idealistic 16-year-old who believed she would be saving humanity by opening the Dome. She should have known better, of course, but she had always been headstrong and idealistic to a fault. The thought of his daughter being kept behind bars for any length of time made him almost physically ill. She'd already been "retrained" in Juvey once before—for only three days—and had returned home looking pale and pounds thinner. "I never want to go back there again," she'd said at the time.

And now this...

The Law Board representative who had accompanied him to the precinct had been no help. Prentiss knew the moment he saw him that the man was a Domer through and through, and thoroughly unsympathetic.

"Be thankful that your daughter is 16 and not an adult," the man told him as they waited to see Violet. "Although for something this serious, there's no telling what the sentence will be."

Prentiss restrained himself from smashing the guy's face from here to Clearpoint View Dome...

Violet had tried to appear strong, even attempting a smile. "Hi, Dad," she'd said when they brought her into the meeting room in handcuffs. But in the harsh S.T.E.P. sudoflicker light, she looked so young, so vulnerable. "Sorry about this. It was stupid. Very stupid." Then her resolve suddenly melted and she began to sob.

"Oh, honey, don't—" Prentiss went to hug her but the woman officer stopped him.

"Please remain seated, sir!" she warned. Then and only then did she remove Vi's handcuffs and allow her to wipe her eyes.

He'd tried to comfort her as best he could. "We'll get through this, I promise. I'm going to see Chief Mulligan after I leave here. Try not to worry, okay?"

"Okay," she nodded. "And I'm sorry, really, really sorry!"

"Time's up!" the woman officer said.

"What? But it's only been ten min—" Prentiss began.

"Time's up!" the officer repeated, louder this time. "You can see her again tomorrow afternoon," she said, slipping the handcuffs back onto Violet's slim wrists.

As Prentiss and the useless Law Board rep started for the door, Violet called:

"Dad! Wait! Tell Mom I love her! Tell my sisters I'm sorry! Tell them I miss them so much..."

That was hours ago. From Juvey he'd gone straight to Chief Mulligan's house, informing the Law Board guy he would no longer require his services. The guy shrugged and muttered under his breath, just loud enough for

Prentiss to hear, "We'll see about that."

It was barely five a.m. Dawn was breaking, or what was supposed to be dawn, anyway. No one alive today had ever seen a real sunrise or a real sunset.

Making his way to Chief Mulligan's house he'd seen no one else on the street. He looked up at the Dome's ceiling, seemingly miles above him. It was incredible that Violet and the others had had the courage to climb such a distance. Yes, *courage*. He thought about it. What if Sunellen and Violet had been right all along, and there really *was* a viable atmosphere beyond the Dome's confines? What if the Board of Presidents—or specifically their own President of West America, Drew Blacker—knew this to be true but for some reason wanted to keep the Dome closed anyway?

He'd never liked President Blacker, and certainly didn't vote for him. He was young—only 67—but he had the political goals of someone much older: "Trust us! Your survival is our priority! Dome safety is everyone's safety!" Those were Blacker's campaign slogans. The population found those promises comforting. This was the same population who'd inherited an earth that had been plundered by people who wouldn't listen to anyone, who had thought Global Warming was just a myth…

Prentiss paused at the Chief's door. He glanced up at the Dome again. Something wasn't right up there. He'd done some cursory checking on his own last week with an OxyNitrometer he'd borrowed from a former colleague over in Sector 9, the area where the mystery virus was currently making an appearance.

No, something wasn't right up there.

Or down here either, he thought with a heavy sigh.

He would have to deal with "down here" now. He hoped with all his being that the Chief of Police would be willing to help him with that.

Chapter 24
VIOLET

She was cold. They kept the temperature in her quadrant at a mere 45°F. She'd asked the guard for an extra blanket and he'd rolled his eyes: "You think you're cold now, you just wait. And no, Miss Big Shot Rebel Triplet Waster, you cannot have an extra blanket! And that's an extra five points on your record just for asking." He waved his scribblewand across his compad and walked back to his post, out of her line of vision, his heels clicking against the simu-tile floor.

"Bloo?" she whispered. Bloo Sycamore was in an adjoining cell, and Violet had heard her coughing all night. "Are you all right? Do you need a nurse?"

"I'm okay," Bloo said.

"You don't sound okay!"

"It's just—well it's so cold in here—" She was interrupted by another coughing spasm.

"Oh, Bloo, I'm so sorry! This whole thing is my fault! I never should have trusted Brink! How could I have been so stupid?!" The thought of Brink Trayor and his betrayal made her feel like screaming, but she couldn't afford such a luxury. She had to be careful not to appear weak to the Juvey guards, to her TBT friends, or even to herself. Most of all to herself!

A loud buzzer interrupted her thoughts. The guard reappeared and unlocked her and Bloo's cell doors. "Both of you—step forward into the corridor!" he commanded. "You kiddies are going to a meeting!"

When Violet stepped into the corridor, the guard shoved her hard enough to make her almost lose her balance. She fell headlong against Bloo, who looked terrified. "Oops—Bloo! I'm sorry!"

"No talking!" the guard yelled, shoving her once again. "Now move!"

They were ushered into a small room and told to sit at a small table in the center. The room was harshly lit, but at least it was warmer in here than in the cell. Violet rubbed her frozen hands together.

A few seconds later, Clinker and Palmer Davis were ushered into the room and ordered to sit at the table without talking. Clinker didn't look too much the worse for wear, but poor Palmer was paler than ever. Violet could see shivers going through his thin body.

"Hey, girls!" Clink said with a wink, and was immediately slammed on the side of the head by the guard.

"I said NO TALKING!" the guard yelled.

At this, Bloo started to cry silently, and the guard threw her a cruel grin which made Violet want to punch him.

Pull yourself together, she ordered herself. She remembered what her father had said when he had visited her earlier: *We'll get through this, I promise.* He was going to see Chief Mulligan to ask him to release her into his custody. Her father could be very convincing, and he had also once saved the Chief's wife, so maybe—

Her thoughts were interrupted by a detective who came in and sat down at the table. "My name is Detective Post," he said, making a point to look everyone in the eye. "It's my job to find out how the Dome's secret mechanism formula and blueprints came to be in your possession. And also whose idea it was initially to commit this serious crime."

Before Violet could say a word, Clinker said, "It was *all* our idea. I mean, we all thought of it. Together."

Detective Post smiled wryly. "Really. The idea to put thousands of innocent lives in danger came to all of you at the same moment. No one person thought of it first?"

Clinker and Bloo nodded uncertainly. Palmer Davis looked down at his hands.

"It was me! I thought up the plan!" Violet exclaimed. "But—but I just put into words what we were all thinking—what we'd all been thinking for a long time," Violet said. She regretted her outburst as soon as the words were out of her mouth.

Detective Post made notes on his compad with his scribblewand. "I see," he said, though it was obvious he didn't see, because his next question was, "And what was it that you were all thinking?"

Violet forced herself to meet his gaze. His eyes were dark and uncomprehending in his broad face. "We were thinking—we know—that Recovery has already begun beyond the Dome! That there's pure, unpolluted air Outside, and that for some reason we're being lied to, and treated like slaves..."

"That's enough!" the detective snapped. His face had turned dark with rage. "You're either lying or unbelievably stupid or both! But it doesn't matter, because you've committed a treasonous act and we're going to get to the truth no matter how long it takes!"

Bloo began to sob harder. Even Clinker looked as if he was about to cry. Palmer sat motionless, staring into his lap.

"And you, Palmer Davis," the detective said. "Like father, like son, eh?"

Violet saw Palmer's face flush bright red.

"My father had nothing to do with this," he said determinedly. There was rebellion in his voice.

Good for you! Violet thought. *Don't let him intimidate you!*

"Except that he's serving a lifetime sentence for committing a similar crime, isn't that true?" the detective said. "Tell me: Did your father somehow slip a copy of the Dome lock formula past the guards in prison? Are you both in collusion with a third party? We know the formula wasn't in your possession until very recently because we searched your house thoroughly at the time of your father's arrest!"

"My father had nothing to do with this!" Palmer said again, but this time his voice wavered a little.

Violet's heart was breaking. Poor Palmer was in all this trouble—they were all in this trouble—because of her and her refusal to see Brink Trayor for the devious spy he was!

Detective Post sat back in his chair. He turned to the guard who'd been sitting silently in a chair by the door. "Take them back to their cells," he said brusquely. "Except for this one." He pointed to Palmer. "I want you to leave this one with me."

Clinker and Bloo shuffled wordlessly to the door. Violet followed. She looked back at Palmer and tried to send him a telepathic signal of support. "Stay strong!" she thought as hard as she could. "We love you! Be brave!"

She had no idea that this would be the last time she would see Palmer Davis alive.

Chapter 25

CHIEF CLIFFORD MULLIGAN

The man pacing back and forth in his study bore little resemblance to the handsome man he'd come to respect and admire. Prentiss Budd seemed drained of energy, worry etched on his normally confident face. "You must do this favor for me, Cliff," he begged.

The Chief shifted uncomfortably in his chair. "Prentiss, you're putting me on the spot. You know I'll be forever grateful to you for saving Augusta—" he paused to clear his throat—"and, of course, myself, after that virus thing. But this—it's a really serious crime, Pren—"

"Don't you think I know that!" Prentiss cut in, loud enough to bring Augusta into the room, still in her nightgown and robe. Prentiss turned to her. "Can't you persuade him?" he begged.

Augusta gave him a sympathetic smile. "Can you persuade NewBlooms to grow for real?" she said with gentle sarcasm. "He's like SumbraSteel. Impervious to everything. Can I get you some NevaTea and a wafer, Prentiss?"

"No thank you," he said, sitting back down in the chair facing the Chief's desk.

When Augusta had left the room, the Chief leaned forward. "It's out of my jurisdiction, Prentiss. Try to understand."

Prentiss glowered at him: "*Nothing* is out of your jurisdiction!" he said brusquely. "One word from you and I could take my daughter home. I promise to keep her with us at all times. Sunellen and I will see to it that Violet won't set foot out of—"

"That's not the point!" the Chief erupted, slamming his hand on the desk. "I could get fired for using my influence in this case! The Board of Presidents could send *me* to jail!" Why couldn't Prentiss understand his position? There weren't many instances he could think of when circumstances made him dislike his job, but this was certainly one of them.

"Since when do you care about the Board of Presidents?" Prentiss asked. "As far as I'm concerned they're all a bunch of—" He let the sentence trail off.

"Listen," he said, lowering his voice. "I need to tell you something. Actually, I'm not even sure you're the one to tell it to. But there's something odd going on with Dome Maintenance. And I have a strong feeling that idiot Drew Blacker is behind it in some way."

The Chief frowned. "What do you mean? What does Dome Maintenance have to do with Violet and her cohorts?" He realized the word, *cohorts*, might have been a poor choice of words when he saw Prentiss' face fall. "Please, Prentiss, say what you mean. I'm confused..."

Prentiss stood abruptly. "You're right. Maybe this isn't the right time." He checked his wrist crystal. "I have to get to the lab." He gave him a stony glare. "If you're unwilling to help in this particular matter, I need to ask another favor from you."

"I'm not *unwilling,* it's just that I'm unable to—"

"I need a Pioneer application. And I need it as soon as possible. Can you help me?"

The Chief stared. Had he heard correctly? "Pioneer...? But I thought you couldn't—I mean, when the triplets were born, you promised to—" he stammered.

"Can you get the application form for me? Yes or no?" Prentiss was scaring him now. He looked angry enough to kill. Not that he ever would, of course. Prentiss Budd was a decent, law-abiding genius of a doctor who had saved untold lives...

"Well?"

"Yes, yes!" the Chief said quickly. "You'll have the application today. I'll hologram it straight to the lab."

Prentiss' expression softened a bit. "Thank you," he said. "But send it to the apartment, not the lab. Tonight." And then he was gone.

Chapter 26

DAISY AND ROSE

The words crawled silently along the bottom of the holoscreen as the news anchor reported on a story about a mystery illness that had been reported in Sector 9: *"Rebel group member kills self in cell,"* the message read. *"Details to follow..."*

Daisy's mother's scream rang through the apartment. "Prentiss!"

"It's not Violet," her father said with certainty. "Violet would never harm herself!!"

He immediately crystal-called the Juvey precinct and demanded to know the identity of the suicide victim. He was told that information was unavailable.

"This is Dr. Prentiss Budd!" he said in a voice so loud it made Pip shiver. "And you will tell me what I want to know or Chief Mulligan will hear about it!" The voice on the other end of the crystal told him to wait.

Daisy ran to her mother and hugged her. "It's not Vi," she assured her. "I think I would know if it were."

"Oh, Daisy," her mother said brokenly. "I hope you're right!"

Rose came into the room, already dressed for school. She'd heard the news and couldn't believe it. Could things get any worse? First, her sister Violet does something that would change their lives for good—or, more likely, for bad. Decker Bliss, the boy she loved and whom she thought loved her, was no longer in her life. And now, a member of Violet's group was dead!

If she had to guess, it was probably Clinker James. Violet had introduced them once, a couple of Domes-Days ago, and he'd struck her as a fidgety, nervous type who couldn't—or wouldn't—meet her eyes.

Her father's sigh of relief filled the room. "It's Palmer Davis," he said, switching off his wrist crystal. "Thank Dome, it's not our Violet."

Daisy watched as her mother began to sob. "That poor child! Why would he do such a thing?" And, "Violet must be blaming herself!"

Her mother was probably right about that, Daisy thought. Violet always blamed herself if things didn't go as planned. But in this case Daisy thought the blame was unwarranted. As bad as things might be, taking your life was never the answer.

"Maybe Rose and Daisy should stay at home today," her father said.

The girls exchanged glances. "Yes!" they said in quick unison.

"No!" Sunellen said. "I don't want them to miss school. They had nothing to do with this." She gave them a no-nonsense stare. "Daisy. Rose. Eat your breakfast wafers and get to school." She turned to Prentiss: "I'm going down to Juvey with you. I'll call Principal Collins and let him know I'll be late to class."

Daisy was proud of her mother's determination. She knew that Violet would have been, too.

Before they left the apartment, their father took them aside: "Try to remain strong. School is not going to be easy for you today. Things may never be easy for you again. At least, not as long as we remain here, in Blue Skies."

"What do you mean, Dad?" Rose asked, her eyes widening in surprise.

"I think I know," Daisy said, studying her father's face. "Are we going Pioneer, Dad?" she whispered.

Her father hugged both of them. He kissed each girl on her forehead. "My girls," he said lovingly. "My smart, wonderful girls." Then, "Come straight home from school. We're having a family meeting tonight."

The walk to school was uneventful. But the moment they reached the school grounds, the girls knew their father had been right: Things were not going to be easy for them.

Kids stood around in tight little groups, snickering as Daisy and Rose passed by. More than a few gave them threatening stares. One girl—Daisy thought it might be Tula Osage, one of Ellis Starr's friends—yelled, "It should have been your sister who killed herself!"

Daisy took a step toward her, emboldened by fury, but Rose restrained her. "Don't give them the satisfaction," Rose said, as they entered the supposed safety of the school.

Daisy watched Rose head in the direction of her first class of the day, "Methodology of Mathematics for

Infants," something she might be interested in teaching once she got her degree from Teachers Academy after high school.

Daisy lacked the patience a teaching career required, although she admired people like her mom and Rose who seemed born to the job. She, herself, was heading for Stimulating Simulant Recipes, one of the prerequisite courses for her admittance to S.F.C.

She passed a group standing before a list that had been posted on the wall outside Principal Collins' office. It held the names of seniors and the schools they would be attending after graduation. As she drew closer, the whispering began, and the group dispersed. *Like I'm contagious, or something*, she thought morosely.

Glancing at the list she read:

Rose Budd: Teaching Academy

Daisy Budd: Simulated Food Centers

Violet Budd: Laws Dominion

A line had been drawn through Vi's name. Daisy wanted to cry. Then she saw:

Sharkey Collins: Relevance Labs

Her heart sank even further. She'd hoped she'd been wrong about Sharkey—that he wasn't the dumb Domer he'd always given the impression of being; that he was actually smarter than he let on. That beneath those golden good looks there lurked a bit of decency. But no decent person would want to work in a Relevance Lab! People who had outlived their usefulness to society—their "relevancy"—were brought there to be experimented on, or worse. And the animals! All those innocent animals being subjected to horrible experiments!

A series of chimes interrupted her thoughts. She reached her next class feeling more hopeless than she'd ever felt in her life.

Chapter 27
SUNELLEN

She was at once happier than she ever remembered being, and sadder than she ever thought possible. Visiting Violet this morning in Juvey detention, seeing how much thinner and depressed she seemed, tore at her heart. "We're doing everything we can to get you out of here," she'd assured Violet. "Dad spoke to Chief Mulligan, and—"

"—And he refused to help, right?" Violet said, turning to her father. But before he could reply, she asked: "Dad? Are they going to try me as an adult? Could I be evaporated for this?"

"Absolutely not!" Prentiss insisted. "Don't even think such a thing!"

Terror clutched at Sunellen's heart. Evaporation was reserved for the very worst criminals—murderers, people who poisoned water supplies, assorted demented souls bent on pillage and destruction. Her Violet was just a child who'd let her ideals get the better of her common sense; they would not—could not—atom-smash her into nothingness!

"But I'm responsible for Palmer's suicide," Violet said miserably. "If only I hadn't—"

"That was not your fault!" Sunellen and Prentiss said at the same time.

Sunellen reached out a hand to comfort her. "No touching!" the S.T.E.P. officer yelled from her position at the door.

"Palmer was a sad, lonely boy," Sunellen said, placating. "His mother going Pioneer and deserting the family, and his father in prison..."

"But—" Violet began.

"Violet!" her father cut in. "Misplaced guilt will solve nothing. I want you to concentrate on the fact that we are going to get you out of here, and soon. I promise."

Sunellen turned to him, surprised by the certainty in his tone. Did he know something she didn't?

"Is there anything we can do for you now, honey?" Sunellen asked.

Violet, pale but still so beautiful, gave her a weak smile. "Two things," she said, lowering her voice. "Dad, Bloo in the next cell has been coughing nonstop. Could you have a look at her?"

Prentiss assured her that he would. "What's the other thing, honey?" he asked.

"Could either of you pay a visit to Palmer's dad? He must be feeling so horrible right now..."

"I was going to do that very thing," Sunellen assured her.

And she did. As soon as they left Juvey, Prentiss headed to the lab and she to Blue Skies Prison in Sector 11.

When she told the S.T.E.P. officer at the main desk that she wished to see Grant Davis, he looked at her suspiciously. "I know you," he said, his small eyes virtually disappearing into slits in his doughy face. "You're the mother of that terrorist, the one who tried to break the Dome!"

Sunellen squared her shoulders. In a steady voice, she repeated: "I wish to see Mr. Davis. That is my right, is it not?"

"Sure, sure," the officer said with a sneer. "In Blue Skies, *everyone* has rights. Even mothers of terrorists!" He pushed a button on his desk and a hologram of a cell block appeared behind him. "Prisoner 48481299 to the communication cell. You've got a visitor!"

The hologram clicked off. "Third floor, left corridor," he said curtly. "Guess you terrorists like to stick together, huh?"

She didn't deign to give a reply; instead, she walked quickly to the hover platform that would take her to the third floor.

If ever there were a ghost who was dead but somehow still alive, that would be Grant Davis. With a complexion so waxen it was nearly translucent, and eyes that were hollow with grief, he took a seat on his side of the visitor's table. "Don't lean toward me or you'll be electrocuted," he said matter of factly, as if he were talking about a hovercycle ride on the Intercom Automation Highway.

"Mr. Davis, I'm Su—"

"I know who you are," he said wearily. "What I don't know is why you're here."

"Mr. Davis," she began, starting to lean toward him but pulling back when she remembered that she might be electrocuted. "I am so sorry for your loss. Palmer was such a sweet—"

"Thank you," he said abruptly. Then, shaking his head, "Please. Palmer was a lot of things but I don't know about 'sweet'. Smart, yes, reckless, yes." He gave her a quizzical stare. "Reckless. Like your daughter. And the rest of those kids with their ideals. Their stupid, pointless ideals..." He broke into deep, heartwrenching sobs.

"Not stupid," she muttered.

He looked up, tears staining his hollow cheeks. "What did you say?"

"I said their ideals were not stupid. I believe in them. You believed in them, too, once, or else you wouldn't be here."

He sighed heavily. "Yes. I held similar ideals. Once." After swiping at his tears with the back of his hand, he added, "Look, I don't blame your daughter for Palmer's suicide, if that's what you think. If it weren't Truth Be Told, my son would have found another group that would get him into trouble."

Sunellen smiled sadly and, after a few seconds of silence, she stood. "Well, I just wanted to let you know how much we—my family and I—regret this tragedy. Goodbye, Mr. Davis." She turned to leave.

"Wait," he said. "Tell your husband if he ever wanted to talk to me about—well, about *things*—I'll gladly help him in any way I can."

Puzzled, Sunellen asked: "What things might those be?"

"Dome things," he whispered. He stood. In another moment he was gone, back to his cell where he was destined to spend the rest of his life.

She'd left the prison feeling depressed and terribly sad. For Grant Davis and for Violet, for their future in Blue Skies.

But that was this morning. Now, tonight, she was feeling hopeful again. Hopeful and even optimistic because, miraculously, Prentiss had had a change of heart!

Because now, with Prentiss and Daisy and Rose seated around the little table in their kitchen, she was looking at something she'd been aching to see for a long, long time: An application for going Pioneer.

Chapter 28

ROSE

It was so ironic! When Decker Bliss was still part of her life, she had stubbornly resisted the idea of leaving Blue Skies. But now, after everything that had happened to her family in the last month, she couldn't wait to start fresh somewhere else. And not just somewhere else, but a whole new world! Hopefully there *was* a world outside the Dome. Hopefully, they wouldn't all die of pollution poisoning or something equally as horrible the moment they left Blue Skies!

Two weeks ago their parents had completed the Pioneer application. There were 20 pages filled with sentences like "State your reason(s) for leaving Blue Skies."

How about, *Ever since my sister got caught trying to open the Dome, life for us has been a nightmare,* she'd thought to herself.

The answer her father gave went something like, "We would like to contribute to the Earth Recovery

Movement that we believe is taking place outside the Dome."

These were the terms they had to accept:

1. "Once you and/or your family leave Blue Skies, any request to re-enter a Domed city will be permanently denied."

2. "No form of communication is possible once you leave Blue Skies (or any other Domed city)."

3. "You agree to vacate your apartment and donate all furnishings to the citizens of Blue Skies."

4. "You agree to pay the Exit Fees of $10,000 per person."

At the very bottom of the application form was a statement that read:

"You agree not to hold any member of the Board of Presidents liable for any death(s) or impairment(s) that may occur to you and/or any family member upon exiting Blue Skies Dome."

Rose worried about that one. "Dad? Are you really sure we should be doing this?"

Her father, ever honest, said: "Look, honey. There's no way we can know for certain what's out there. Your mom and I want you to understand that we'll be taking a big risk by leaving. If you feel you'd rather not take that chance, then we'll stay here."

Daisy said, "I don't think dying could be much worse than what we face every day by staying here. Don't you agree, Rose?"

She did agree. The clamor about Violet had not died down as they'd hoped it would. She and Daisy were still being greeted by stares and insults at school, especially by Ellis Starr and her clique. Even their neighbors here in the building went out of their way to avoid them. And although they had never felt truly accepted—they were a family of triplets, after all—Violet's attempt to open the Dome was simply the last straw in the view of the Dome population.

Rose said, "What about Violet? We're not leaving without her, are we?"

"Of course not!" her father had almost shouted. Then, lowering his voice, he added, "I'm fairly certain we'll have Violet out of detention in a matter of weeks."

But was fairly certain good enough? In a small voice, Rose said, "Well, I'm not leaving without her."

"Nor I," said Daisy.

"Nor I," said her mother. Then they all giggled nervously at the ridiculousness of leaving one of their own behind.

Because her dad always seemed so sensitive about his promise never to leave the Dome in exchange for letting her stay born, Rose hesitated before she asked: "Dad— how sure are you that the Board of Presidents will allow you to leave?"

"Very sure," he said. "Very sure indeed."

Chapter 29

VIOLET

They were not allowed to take their meals with the rest of the Juvey population. "We don't want your poisonous rhetoric influencing the other losers," was how one of the S.T.E.P. guards put it.

She, Bloo and Clinker ate in the tiny, windowless room opposite the main hall. There they were told they were permitted to talk.

Who were they kidding? Violet thought. The room was riddled with invisible listening waves. Every word they said could be heard by the detectives who *wanted* them to talk, in order to find out whatever Brink hadn't already told them.

Only two members of TBT had managed to elude capture and were hiding out; all the rest of the group had been caught and placed in a detention center in a different sector.

"I can't eat this," Violet said, pushing away her platter of lunch wafers. The food in Juvey contained no flavor enhancers whatsoever. It was like eating NeuFab. "We might as well just peel the walls," she said.

Clinker frowned. "You've got to keep your strength up," he said, stuffing a wafer into his mouth and grimacing. "Mmm, delicious!" he proclaimed loudly, knowing the police were listening to every word.

This made Bloo giggle, and she nibbled at her wafer. "Yum!" she nodded. "Just like homemade!"

Bloo looked terrible. Her eyes were red-rimmed, and her complexion was sallow. Violet's father had been rebuffed when he'd asked to examine her months ago after they'd been apprehended. "We have our own medical staff," a guard insisted.

"But I'll bet they're not all good friends of Chief Mulligan," he'd retorted. "Now unlock that child's cell at once!"

He'd given Bloo a shot of Immunall and her cough had disappeared immediately. He'd also requested a second blanket for Bloo, Clinker and herself, which they also, reluctantly, agreed to.

"Your father is so wonderful," Bloo said now. "I envy you."

Violet smiled. "Thank you," she said softly. "He is pretty great as fathers go, I guess." She immediately regretted her words, remembering too late that Bloo's own parents had officially discarded her after she'd been arrested.

"Hey," Clinker said, trying for a light tone. "Who wants to hear a joke?"

"No one," she and Bloo said together. This made them all giggle a little.

"Violet, I'm still hungry. Are you gonna eat those wafers?" Clink asked.

Violet rolled her eyes. "Be my guest," she said, dropping the limp things onto his plate. She sighed. "I can't stop thinking about Palmer..." Her breath caught in her throat and she used all her willpower to keep the tears at bay. "I feel so responsible!"

Bloo looked at her questioningly: "Don't tell me you blame yourself for his suicide!"

"But I do! If it hadn't been for me..."

Bloo reached out to touch her. "No touching!" said the beefy woman guard who stood by the door.

Bloo's hand went back into her lap. "Vi, listen to me! Don't you know that the reason he killed himself was..." she glanced at the guard, who was watching them intently. She lowered her voice to the barest whisper: "Palmer was trying to protect his father! Palmer knew he'd be tortured and then his father might be tempted to disclose..." She covered her mouth with her hands to shield against lip-reading: "His dad knows secret stuff about the Dome mechanism! That's why they're listening to every word we're saying! They think we might know, too!"

Violet looked at Clinker, who nodded.

"It's true," he whispered. "When Palmer hung himself, he took everything he knew with him."

Violet remembered that Palmer's father had once been a respected chemical engineer. He'd even been a member of the Dome Maintenance Committee until, soon after the new Board of Presidents was elected five years ago, he'd suddenly been arrested for trying to sabotage the Dome's locking mechanism.

Just then two burly S.T.E.P. officers burst into the room: "On your feet!" one of them yelled at Bloo. "You two," he said to Clinker and Violet, "You stay seated!"

They cuffed Bloo's hands behind her back and dragged her to the door.

"What's going on?!" Violet yelled, standing. "What'd she do?!"

"Sit down!" the fat, ugly guard screamed.

"Today's my birthday!" Bloo called out miserably. "I'm 17! I'm no longer considered a juvenile!" She broke into tears.

"Yeah. Happy birthday, rebel!" one of the officers said with an evil grin.

"Holy Dome!" Clinker breathed. All the color had left his face. Looking at Violet, he asked: "My 17th's not until next month. When's yours?"

Violet's heart was beating crazily in her chest. "In three weeks," she said, feeling dizzy. "In three weeks I'll be considered an adult, too."

The age of majority—when criminals could be tried as adults—had been 18 until five years ago, when the new Board of Presidents had lowered it to 17. She'd heard that their own president, Drew Blacker of West America, had spearheaded the new law. Lance Stickers from the

South district had applauded it. The other half of the board, River Robles from the North and Ruby Jewell from the East, had had some reservations, but in the end, they'd given in to the pressure and the law had passed.

Violet remembered from her Ancient Modern History class that at one time, hundreds of years ago, just one president was elected to run the entire country. It was such a primitive idea! How could one person be expected to oversee so many millions of people? Back then they'd had something called Congress, and there were Sentries—no, wait—Senators!—who were supposed to represent individual states.

She remembered reading that people held conflicting views about the Warming, which they also called Climate Change. Many never believed it could happen, until one day the mega floods and droughts could no longer be denied.

But by then, it was too late to do anything about it.

Later that night, alone in her freezing cell, the two thin blankets pulled up tightly under her chin, Violet cried for Bloo. When their trial began—and no one knew exactly when that might be—Bloo would be tried as an adult. If found guilty, she could be evaporated. Soon—*too soon*—the same fate would befall her and Clink.

She shivered. Her parents, who visited every day, kept saying she'd be released into their custody very soon. But how long would that be?

Only a miracle could save her now, she thought in desperation. And she didn't believe in miracles.

Chapter 30

SHARKEY COLLINS

He thought Daisy Budd and her sister, Rose, were the bravest people he'd ever known. That went for their mom, Mrs. Budd, too. None of them had missed a single day at school since Violet Budd pulled that stunt with her crazy pals. Granted, Mrs. Budd had been coming to school late most mornings because she visited Violet down at Juvey, but he couldn't fault her for that. He wondered if his father would be so loyal if *he* ever pulled such a stunt. Not that he ever would, of course.

Sharkey loved his father, but lately he'd started to question the old man's values. "Stay away from Wasters," his father always told him. "They're troublemakers. Stick with your own kind, son, and you'll never regret it."

But Sharkey was regretting it already. After the incident with Violet Budd, his father had become obsessed with the Budds: "That family is a menace to society!" he'd ranted. "Under present law, I can't legally fire Sunellen for her daughter's treasonous act, but I would like nothing better!" He peered suspiciously at Sharkey: "And that reminds me: I've heard a rumor about you and that other Budd girl—Daisy, is it? You've been seen talking with her at school. Is that true?"

Sharkey frowned. "Well, yeah. I mean—it's not against the law to talk to a Wa... I mean, a girl who *hasn't* broken any law, is it? At least not yet, anyway!"

"Watch that tone, son!" his father warned. "Now get busy and study up on those Relevance Lab bylaws. You'll be working there in less than a month."

Don't remind me, Sharkey thought. He didn't really want to work in a Relevance Lab, but he had no idea what else he might do with his life. If he were smarter, he might want to be a doctor and help people, even though in 2275 most diseases had been eradicated. He thought about Daisy's father, Dr. Budd, and how gratifying it must have been to have helped find the cure for cancer. How proud his family must be, even though they were Wa...

He stopped himself. He really should stop using that word, *Waster*. Dr. Budd had contributed hugely to society. Mrs. Budd was a great teacher, and Rose Budd would probably be a great one, too. And Daisy...ah, beautiful Daisy; it wasn't her fault that her sister Violet was a terrorist. And that was another question he'd been asking himself: Did "terrorist" really apply here? Was anyone really sure that opening the Dome would spell death for everyone living under it? Suppose the rebels were right and the air Outside was no longer polluted by all those greenhouse gases from the Warming? Suppose Earth's recovery had already begun and the Pioneers had it right all along?

His head started to throb with all these questions that seemed to have no answer.

He opened the book he'd been given after being accepted into the Relevance Lab in Sector 4, which was a good distance from his apartment. He'd have to get up pretty early to get to work on time. On the other hand, Sector 4 was where Daisy lived. Maybe they'd run into each other sometime, he on his way to the Relevance Lab, she on her way to the Simulated Food Center.

He glanced down at the cover of the book in his lap: "Rules and Bylaws of Relevance Lab Sector 4, Blue Skies Dome, Volume 57, January 2275." He opened it to the first chapter: "Maintaining Objectivity, Animal vs. Human Subjects."

After nearly an hour, he hadn't read past the first paragraph. All he could think about was Daisy Budd, how beautiful she was, and what it would be like to kiss her.

Chapter 31

PRENTISS

He frowned at the holographic application hanging in the air in front of him. Stamped in big red lettering across the front, it read, "APPLICATION DENIED." Each member of the Board of Presidents had signed it. Prentiss had expected this, but disappointment flooded him anyway. Always the optimist, he'd hoped the powers that be might forgive and forget about his 17-year-old promise to never leave Blue Skies. At the very least, he hoped they might grant him some leeway for his contribution to society with the invention of Genocell.

He was dealing with other disappointments as well. Chief Mulligan's refusal to help still rankled. Then there was the mysterious disappearance of his good friend, Bill Simmons, his colleague over in Rainbow Arc. He'd tried to reach him by crystal-calling, holotext, and even scribblegramming, but no luck.

Yesterday, he'd left work half a day early and driven a monorail battery cart down the Interdome Automation Highway all the way to Rainbow Arc. The two-hour trip ended in frustration, for when he reached Bill's lab, the only other researcher working there said she hadn't seen Bill Simmons in over a month and had no idea where he might be.

He'd wanted to talk to Bill about the anomaly he'd found while checking the atmospherics of the Dome. Last week, he'd risen before dawn and gone to Sector 7, where the "mystery virus" was now giving people headaches. He'd taken air samples with his detrax pump and gone directly back to the lab to analyze them in detail. Sure enough, the oxygen level, which should have been 20 percent, was down to only 19.4 percent! It was common knowledge that oxygen levels lower than 19.5 percent could have deleterious effects on the human brain. The other components seemed normal enough— 78.084 percent nitrogen, carbon dioxide 0.033 percent, argon 0.934 percent. The traces of methane were slightly higher than they should be but he didn't think that was a problem.

The really stunning thing, however, was that when he measured the air quality in his own sector, Sector 4, the oxygen component was completely normal! It was as if the levels were deliberately being manipulated from one sector to another, and it answered the question of why all the sectors were not affected at the same time. Was this something to talk to Dome Maintenance about? After all, it was their responsibility—the most important job under the Dome—to see that the air quality being filtered into Blue Skies was absolutely perfect at all times.

But before he took any action on his own, he wanted to ask Bill Simmons if he was encountering anything like this over in Rainbow Arc. He knew Bill could be trusted with inquiries like these. He also knew he could *not* trust people like Harlan Cedars, his lab colleague, who seemed to derive sadistic pleasure from reporting patients to Relevance Labs after they'd come down with the virus.

Speaking of which, Harlan entered the lab at that very moment. Casting a sidelong glance his way, he said, "Dr. Budd. Early again, I see." He made it sound like an accusation.

Prentiss quickly switched off the hologram of the rejected Pioneer Application and locked it into his computer storage bin. He used his private security code to keep it there. "Making up for yesterday," he said casually, not bothering to look up.

"Ah, yes," Harlan said. "By the way, how are things going with your daughter? The one in Juvenile Deten—"

"They're going as well as can be expected," Prentiss cut in. "By the way, I'll be leaving early today, too. Have to visit an old friend who's not well."

"Oh?" said Harlan, "Another case of the virus?"

Prentiss shrugged. "Won't know until I examine him," he said, careful to lock his desk drawers. He *really* didn't trust Harlan. "Carla should be in soon, so I think you two will be able to manage without me."

"Oh, I'm sure we will," Harlan said. "And please call me if there's anything I can do to help your daughter, the one in detention."

"Absolutely," Prentiss said, thinking, *"Not even if I ran out of every option would I consider calling you."*

Until this moment, he wasn't sure he would visit the father of that dead boy, Palmer Davis, in prison. He'd gotten the impression that Grant Davis must be some sort of fool to try to mess with the Dome mechanism. It was one thing if you were an idealistic teenager like Violet and her group, but Davis was a grown man when he'd committed his crime, a respected chemist who worked with the Dome Maintenance Committee!

"I have a feeling he has some worthwhile information to offer," Sunellen said after she'd visited him in jail.

"What does that even mean?" he'd asked impatiently. "What information could a misguided individual like Grant Davis possibly have to offer us?"

"I don't think he's misguided at all," she said softly, fixing her blue-eyed imploring gaze on him, a gaze he could never resist.

So here he was, making his way to the third-floor corridor of Blue Skies prison in Sector 11, to meet with the father of a dead friend of Violet's.

The whole business made him feel uncomfortable. He was already wishing he hadn't come.

He couldn't know it then, but for the rest of his life, he would be grateful that he did.

Chapter 32

DAISY AND ROSE

They ran into each other on the way to class: Daisy to Ancient Music of the Late 20th Century with Mr. Jagger, and Rose to Calculus for Toddlers with Miss Numbra, whose classroom was right next door.

Daisy was worried about Rose. She looked as though she'd been crying again. Rose was doing a lot of crying these days. The whole family was upset about what happened to Violet, and everyone was nervous about getting her out of Juvey in time to go Pioneer, but Rose seemed to be taking it the hardest.

"What's going on?" Daisy whispered, giving Rose a brief hug. "You look as though the world has ended."

Rose flashed her beautiful green eyes at Daisy. "It might as well have," she sighed. "I was actually starting to look forward to..."—and here she looked around to make sure no one was within earshot—"...you know, going Pioneer, but now that the application was denied, I—"

"But didn't you hear Dad say that would be no problem? That we should still count on leaving just as soon as Violet is released into our custody?"

Rose shook her head and her burnished red hair glinted in the sudoflicker light of the school corridor. "I think Dad's just saying that to make us all feel better. I don't think they'll ever let Violet out of jail! And I never heard of anyone going Pioneer after their application has been rejected, have you?"

Daisy shook her head. "No. But that's because it's not something anyone would exactly brag about, NewBloom brain!" She meant this as a gentle tease, but to her horror Rose began to sob. "Rose! What is it? What's really bothering you?"

Rose's next words were practically incoherent, but it sounded like she was saying, "It's all my fault!"

"What? *What's* all your fault?"

Kids were giving them curious glances as they hurried to their classes. The chimes would sound any nanosec. Rose looked up with a brokenhearted stare: "Don't you know? *I'm* to blame—me, Rose, the last of the triplets!

If I hadn't stayed born, you and Violet would have had it so much easier!"

The chimes interrupted. Daisy was shocked. Had Rose been grappling with guilt all these years? *Misguided* guilt, as their Dad would have put it. "But Mom and Dad wanted you so much—" Someone jostled her elbow.

"Move it, Waster!" None other than Ellis Starr.

"What did you call her?" Rose erupted with sudden fury.

"I called her a Wa—"

Before Ellis could finish the word, Rose was on her, pummeling her with her fists and finally knocking her down. Rose fell heavily on top of her. "Don't you ever say that word to my sister again, do you hear me!"

Ellis, eyes wide with surprise (and, Daisy was certain, a goodly amount of pain, because her left eye was already puffing out to the size of a giant apple wafer) seemed too stunned to say a word.

A crowd was gathering. A mostly stupefied crowd: Rose Budd, the "quiet" triplet, was beating up on Ellis Starr, the "tough" girl with the smart mouth!

Daisy tried to get Rose to stop the pummeling. "Rose, enough! You'll kill her!" But Rose was beyond hearing. Ellis's jaw made a cracking sound as it met with Rose's right fist. "Owwwwww!" Ellis screamed. "Get her off me!" It sounded like, "wwwooogroffee".

Then Mr. Jagger was there, trying his best to pry Rose loose, except that Rose still had her fist entangled in Ellis' short black hair. When Mr. Jagger pulled, so did Rose. And when Rose was finally standing, Ellis' hair was still in her hand.

A gasp erupted from the crowd. Daisy's head was spinning and the corridor began to tilt a little.

"Holy Dome!" Mr. Jagger whispered under his breath, his eyes wide with horror.

"Cracklin' Neufab!" someone in the crowd shouted. "She's wearing a wig! Ellis Starr has no hair!"

Rose and Daisy exchanged disbelieving glances.

Was it possible? Was Ellis a victim of those tainted CPC fertility chemicals that were sabotaged 16 years ago? Daisy had heard about this. The fetuses that didn't die from the poisoned batch of chemicals had other

176

things wrong with them: Missing limbs, no eyes, bad hearing, and, in some cases, no hair. The ones with missing limbs and no eyes were evaporated immediately, but Daisy imagined that hiding baldness was relatively easy. For all she knew, there could be other classmates with the same condition. And as long as they didn't make Rose angry, their secret would be safe!

Daisy couldn't help it. She started to giggle. Rose looked at her and began to giggle as well. Soon the entire crowd was convulsed with laughter. Even the usually humorless Miss Numbra, who had emerged from her Calculus for Toddlers classroom to see what all the fuss in the corridor was about, tried unsuccessfully to hide a smile.

Mr. Jagger helped Ellis to a sitting position. Wordlessly, Rose handed him Ellis' hair. "Thanks," he said, putting it back on Ellis' bald head, where it sat crookedly.

"You're welcome," Rose said. Then she and Daisy turned away from the scene and, walking arm in arm, let their laughter begin anew.

Chapter 33

VIOLET

She didn't know whether to laugh or cry. How could this be? In the little room where she and Clinker took their meals, the very same room that was riddled with invisible listening waves so that their every word could be heard by the police, Daisy and Rose sat across from them at the table, quietly eating their lunch. Or pretending to.

Daisy grimaced. "How can you eat this stuff? There's no flavoring in this wafer at all!" She dropped the lunch wafer back on her plate with a groan.

"Tell me again what you two Neufab-brains did to land you in here?"

A slow smile began to spread on Rose's face. She gave a sidelong glance to Daisy and the two of them started to giggle.

"This is funny to you?" Violet said incredulously.

"Well, actually, yes." Daisy said. "You should have been there. You wouldn't have recognized Rose."

"—Or Ellis," Rose added, breaking into hysterical laughter.

"Quiet!!!" barked the S.T.E.P. guard who was standing by the door.

This provoked another bout of giggles. "Sorry!" Rose said, trying hard to suppress a smile.

"Wipe that grin off your face or I'll wipe it off for you!" the guard yelled, making a threatening gesture with her fist. At this, Rose paled slightly.

"Ellis had it coming," Daisy said defensively. "She's always gone out of her way to be nasty to me. To us. I'm proud of Rose, Violet. I thought you'd be, too."

"*I'm* proud of her," said Clinker, as he shoved the last lunch wafer into his mouth. "Ellis Starr is nothing but a Fossil Fueler!"

The girls looked up in surprise. That was a pretty raunchy insult. Rose threw him a wide grin. "Thanks!" she said.

"I'm proud, too, I guess," Violet admitted. "But— how many points on your record did this earn you?"

"Twenty. Each. And three days here, in Juvey." Rose shrugged, as if to say, "no big deal".

Daisy said, "Who cares? We'll all be going Pi—"

Violet kicked her sharply under the table. "Quiet!" she whispered. "They're listening to everything we say!"

"Ow!" Daisy moaned, rubbing her leg.

Clinker looked up with a questioning expression. "Excuse me. Did I miss something?"

Violet avoided his eyes. She hadn't said anything to Clink about her family's plans to go Pioneer because, one, she didn't want him to feel as if she were deserting him and, two, the family's application to leave Blue Skies had been denied, so how could her dad believe they'd be going at all?

More worrisome was the fact that if, by some miracle, (and she didn't believe in miracles) they did manage to leave Blue Skies, there wasn't much time. In two weeks she and her sisters would turn 17, which meant she'd be removed from Juvey and placed in tight security in the adult prison. Where Bloo was right this moment, probably feeling terrified.

The door to their little room swung open and Glacier Starr strode in. "Lunchtime's over!" he said in a mean voice. "Stand up and move to the door!"

"But—" Rose began.

"But what!" Glacier barked, moving toward her.

Rose looked shaken. "But I haven't finished my lunch?" she said weakly.

"Oh, I'd say you're finished, all right," Glacier said. "You're the Fossil Fueler who hurt my cousin, aren't you?" he snarled, thrusting his face inches from Rose's.

Violet saw Clinker's muscles tense. She knew that in any other situation, Clink would have punched Glacier clear to Rainbow Arc, as would she. But one doesn't fight with guards when one is a prisoner.

Violet watched in amazement as Rose stood tall and squared her shoulders. She smiled widely at Glacier, and tossed her beautiful, long red hair in what could only be described as a defiant gesture.

"Yes," she said. "That was me. Sending your bald cousin to the hospital. Would you like my scribble-wand autograph?"

Glacier turned as red as the simulated sun that hung high in the roof of Blue Skies Dome. The rules of Juvey forbade guards to physically assault prisoners, at least while another guard was watching. Violet was thankful that Rose would be here for only two more days.

And yes, Violet thought, she was proud! Proud that Rose had finally found her inner strength and proud that she had acted on it.

I love you, my sister, Violet tried to message her telepathically. *My beautiful, strong, fearless sister!*

Chapter 34
PRENTISS

He had felt the burden of responsibility many times in the past, but never as heavily as now, as he sat facing President Drew Blacker. The well-being of his family was at stake: Violet's release from Juvey, their plans for going Pioneer—their very future—depended on the outcome of this meeting. He would have to tread carefully in very dangerous waters.

"Thank you for seeing me on such short notice, Mr. President," he said, in what he hoped was a respectful tone.

Blacker lifted his hands palms up in a conciliatory gesture. "I could do no less for the person who developed the cure for cancer," he said, smiling his public smile.

"Thank you, sir, but it was my *team* who developed Genocell, not just myself..."

"Modesty. How refreshing. Now, what was that important information you said you could disclose to no one other than me?"

Prentiss did his best not to betray his dislike of the man. Everything about him rang false. Blacker was slender and tall, with high cheekbones and shiny black hair. He might have been considered handsome were it not for an aura of sleaze that clung to him like a polluted cloud. "Well, it has to do with the atmosphere in our Dome." Prentiss' words seemed to echo in the silence that followed.

"I—I'm not sure what you mean," Blacker stammered, his eyes narrowing. "What about the atmosphere in our Dome?"

"It's tainted," Prentiss stated simply. He watched with satisfaction as the color drained from Blacker's face.

"What?" Blacker said, with a grin that was more like a grimace. "Oh, come now, Dr. Budd! You must be mistaken! Our Dome Maintenance Committee would never allow—"

"I've spoken to Grant Davis," Prentiss said sharply. "He told me everything." He was sure his heartbeat could be heard in the nanoseconds it took for Blacker to find his voice.

"Grant Davis?" Blacker repeated, his eyes narrowing. "What does that traitor have to do with—"

"I have the tape!" Prentiss interrupted again.

"Tape? What tape?" Blacker said nervously. "Look, Dr. Budd, whatever it is you think you know it'll have to wait. I have a meeting with President Stickers in 10 minutes. If you'll make another appointment..." He pushed his chair back and stood. Prentiss noticed how his hand shook slightly as he reached for the intercom on his desk.

"You might want to hear what I have to say before you do that," Prentiss said, lowering his voice.

President Blacker hesitated and, slowly, sank back into his chair. And, for the next half hour, he listened wordlessly to all that Prentiss was prepared to tell him.

Two Days Earlier:

"They did it for the money." Grant Davis took a long drink of his NevaTea before he continued, speaking so softly at times that Prentiss could barely hear him. More than once he'd started to lean in across the table and Davis would have to remind him about the danger of being electrocuted if he got too close.

"The idea was to keep raising the Dome taxes while reducing the costs of maintaining the filtering system. The Maintenance Committee members wanted higher salaries. The suppliers were constantly raising the cost of transmitting the air components. Blacker's idea was to skimp on the oxygen. Not all at once, just a little here and there, skipping sectors to make it harder to tell what was happening." He shrugged. "It might have worked, too, if I hadn't spoiled his plans."

Prentiss couldn't believe what he was hearing. How could he have misjudged Davis so badly, thinking he was a fool when, in reality, he was just trying to prevent a disaster?

"So you confronted President Blacker?"

"Not just Blacker. But that other scoundrel too, Lance Stickers, from the South. They were in it together. I don't think the other presidents had a clue, up there in the North and East Districts."

"So you told them you wouldn't go along with their plan?" Prentiss asked. "How did they react?"

"They reacted by framing me! By saying that I'd tried to sabotage the Dome mechanism! I'd gone to the Dome controls after the maintenance crew left for the day, planning to reset the oxygen levels back to normal. They probably figured I'd be dumb enough to do something like that and they were waiting for me." He took another long swig of simulated tea.

"Unbelievable," Prentiss breathed. "But—wait—this was five years ago, when Blacker and Stickers were first elected. The brain damage symptoms from lack of oxygen only manifested itself a few months ago..."

"They got scared," Grant Davis said. "They threw me in prison and decided to wait and see if anyone else would spoil their little scheme. Guess they thought it was safe to try again."

Prentiss said nothing for awhile as he let everything sink in. Grant Davis had a spectral, haunted look about him, the look of a decent man who'd been framed for a crime he hadn't committed. A man who'd lost his only son under horribly coincidental circumstances.

"How do I stop them?" Prentiss asked. "Without proof, no one will believe this."

"Oh, I have proof," Davis said. An ironic smile tried and failed to bring light to his sad eyes.

Then he told Prentiss about the holograph he'd secretly taped at one of the meetings between President Blacker and the Dome Maintenance Committee. It was one of the final meetings where they discussed the schedule to decide which sector would get the lesser amount of oxygen, and when.

"There were a couple of people on the committee who didn't like the plan," Grant Davis said. "Didn't like it at all. But they were smart enough to keep their doubts to themselves. Unlike me." He shook his head ruefully.

The tape was embedded in the copy of a book that could be found in the Library of Antiquities, on Water Street in Sector 11. Prentiss knew exactly where that building was; he'd gone there on many occasions when he was researching a cure for cancer. He wanted to study the prevailing cancer treatments of 200 years ago. The methods were barbaric, to say the least; pumping humans full of ghastly chemicals and dousing them with radiation in the hopes of killing tumors. More often than not, the treatments killed patients before the disease did.

When he arrived at the library, he asked the librarian where he might find a book called *The Life of Richard Nixon*. Nixon had been a United States president (when there was only one president to oversee the entire nation!) way back in the 1970s. Some said he suffered from a lack of personal and political integrity.

Nice touch, Grant Davis, he thought to himself.

There'd been some scary moments when the librarian had scanned and rescanned the stacks of holographic files and nothing had come up. "Hmmm—I don't think—oh, wait! Yes, here it is!" She'd looked at Prentiss with a puzzled expression. "Who was Richard Nixon?" she'd asked.

"That's what I'm going to find out," he told her.

He'd taken the book home where he and Sunellen had followed Grant Davis' instructions on how to extract the tape from the holographic text. And suddenly, right there in their little living room, stood President Drew Blacker and the members of the Dome Maintenance Committee, discussing the details of which sector would receive the reduced oxygen and when.

Now President Blacker was watching himself, too. Watching in silence at his holographic image of wrongdoing. He looked pale now, sitting hunched in his chair.

"Seen enough, Mr. President?" Prentiss asked.

"Switch that thing off!" Blacker hissed. Then, in barely controlled fury: "What is it you want, Dr. Budd? Money? How much? I'll give you—"

"Not money," Prentiss said in a commendably even tone. "I wish to be released from my old promise to remain in Blue Skies. My family and I want to leave for the Pioneer areas as soon as we can."

The relief on Blacker's face was palpable. "Done!" he nodded. He called for an aide to bring in a blank Pioneer Application and signed his name at the bottom. "There! Now, no matter what information you provide, the application will be accepted."

He handed the signed application to Prentiss and reached out his other hand as if to receive the tape.

"There's one more thing," Prentiss said.

Hatred filled Blacker's eyes. Prentiss felt sure that Blacker would have killed him on the spot if he could. And he might still, Prentiss thought chillingly, if he weren't careful. "And what might that one more thing be, Dr. Budd?"

"I want my daughter, Violet Budd, to be released from juvenile detention immediately."

Confusion momentarily clouded the president's face. "Detention? I'm not sure I understand—" A knowing sneer twisted his mouth into a semblance of a smile. "Oh. Right. That rebel group—the ones who tried to open the D..." He stopped before he could complete the word.

He sat back down in his chair. "Well, now, Dr. Budd, I'm not sure I can agree to—"

Prentiss pressed a button on his crystal watch and suddenly a holograph of Sunellen appeared in the room. "This is my wife, Sunellen Budd," Prentiss said. "Hi, honey." Sunellen waved wordlessly. "As you can see, Sunellen is holding the holotape, Mr. President. The tape you wouldn't want the news media to see. Now she's positioning it into the message slot on our crystal-call phone. This would send the tape to every news bureau in every Domed city in the nation in a matter of seconds." He paused. "So, Mr. President. When can I expect to have my daughter back in my custody?"

It took a moment or two before the President could speak. But Prentiss had already waited so long for Violet's release. He supposed he could wait a few seconds longer.

Chapter 35

VIOLET

"Wake up! Move it, Budd!"

Someone was poking her in the ribs, poking hard enough to make her cry out with pain.

"Owww! What—?" She opened her eyes to find Glacier Starr and another officer whose name she did not know bending over her floor mat.

"Get up! We're moving you out of Juvey!" Glacier yelled, his face inches from hers. His breath smelled like stale beer wafer and she almost gagged.

They were moving her out of Juvey! Her father must have accomplished the impossible—she would be released into his custody! A minute later, however, when Glacier snapped handcuffs on her and began pushing her toward the cell door, she knew she'd been wrong. "Wait—where are you taking me?" she said, unable to keep the fear out of her tone.

"We're taking you where you belong, where you should have been taken in the first place—to adult prison!"

"But—you can't! My birthday isn't for another three days! I'm still 16!!" she protested, trying as hard as she could to resist. It was no use. With an officer on each side, they dragged her out of her cell into the dim sudoflicker light of the corridor. Where Ellis Starr, in her green S.T.E.P. Trainee uniform, stood watching the proceedings with a grin. Violet could see the yellowing bruise around her left eye, and the jaw which was still slightly out of alignment with the rest of her face.

Violet felt a jolt of pride, knowing that her sister, Rose, had left her mark. She couldn't help herself: "Hi, Ellis. How's your hair these days?"

Ellis took a threatening step toward her but was swiftly restrained by the officer on her right: "Hold it! Not now! We have to get her to the prison in one piece, Chief's orders."

"Just you wait, Waster," Ellis hissed. "You wait till I graduate. I'll pay you a visit in prison you won't forget!"

"Looking forward to it," Violet said, forcing a smile. "Just use stronger glue on your wig when you do."

Ellis lurched, and in less than a nanosec was able to land a punch to Violet's chest, hard enough to knock the breath out of her. Violet fell against Glacier, who stumbled backwards and smacked into the wall. Bits of Neufab flaked onto the floor. "Ellis! For Dome's sake!" he yelled. "Give it a rest!"

"I'm gonna get her if it's the last thing I do!" she promised. "I'm gonna..."

"WHAT'S GOING ON HERE!" The booming voice of Chief Mulligan startled them all.

Glacier, a surprised look on his face, sputtered, "Sir, Chief Mulligan, sir, I don't—I'm sorry, things just..."

"That trainee hit me!" Violet managed, still fighting for a breath.

Chief Mulligan frowned at Ellis. "You accosted a prisoner? Don't you know that's against the rules?"

Ellis seemed to wither under his gaze. "I'm sorry, sir, but she was acting up, she was resisting—"

"That's 10 points on your record!" Peering at the tag on her jacket which read, "Starr, Ellis, Intern-Trainee", he said, "Report to me in my office before you leave this building, Miss Starr!"

"Yes, sir," Ellis murmured, her face now as red as a fake sunset under the Dome.

Chief Mulligan told Glacier and the other officer to leave. "I'll escort this prisoner to adult prison myself!"

"Are you sure, sir?" Glacier said nervously. "She's a wild one!"

"I think I can manage," he replied with a touch of sarcasm. "Now go! Don't you two have other work to do?!"

"Yes, sir!" they replied simultaneously.

"How are you doing, Violet?" Chief Mulligan said as soon as they had gone. His tone was caring as he gently led her down the corridor to—well, she had no idea exactly where they were going.

"I guess I'm fine—my chest hurts—" she paused and looked up at him. He wasn't a handsome man but there was kindness in his eyes. "Do you know me?"

"I'm a friend of your father's," he said. "I've known all *about* you for years. And your sisters, too. Your father is a very proud man."

She had to smile at that. "Yes he is," she said, thinking, *not too proud to ask you for help which you refused...*

He led her to a small room at the end of the corridor. The sign on the door read: "Prisoner Transfer Room." He closed the door behind them and locked it.

Terror was mounting in her. "I tried to tell them!" she sputtered. "I'm still 16—until next week, at least—I don't want to go to adult prison, Chief Mulligan, I beg you, please—will you let me talk to my father...?"

He seemed not to be listening. He guided her to a chair and motioned her to sit. "You're not going to adult prison," he said in a near-whisper. "I've got to leave these handcuffs on you for the time being, and you may have to wait here for a while—perhaps for as long as a whole day—but I need you to keep calm. Do you understand?"

She didn't, actually. But his tone was so gentle that the fear within her began to subside. She watched as he opened a drawer and removed a cup of desalinated water and a plate of dessert wafers which he set on the table before her. He pointed to a corner of the room: "The bathroom is over there and I think you can manage with the cuffs on. I've told everyone that you're a dangerous, out-of-control prisoner and no one is to have contact with you except myself. It will be my responsibility alone to see that you get transported safely."

"Transported where?" she asked in a shaky voice. "Where will you be taking me?"

If his warm smile was meant to comfort her, it did. "You'll know soon enough," he said. Before he left, she heard him mutter under his breath, "Dangerous, out-of-control prisoner indeed!" He laughed softly to himself and, to her credit, she found herself smiling as well.

Chapter 36

SUNELLEN

"Maybe it's a mistake to go," Sunellen said. "Maybe it would be better for all of us if we just stayed right here in Blue Skies."

The three of them—Prentiss, Daisy and Rose—looked at her as if she'd suddenly lost her mind. Well, maybe she had, just a little. The events of the past week would be enough to test anyone's sanity. First Daisy and Rose had been arrested for attacking that Starr girl; they were placed in Juvey which meant, if only for a few days, all three of her girls had been incarcerated at the same time!

Then came the incident with President Blacker. Prentiss had taken an enormous risk in blackmailing him with the tape of his corruption. Blacker was known to have an explosive temper and Prentiss could have been arrested on the spot, or worse...

She shuddered. Now that their application had been granted—and in record-breaking time, she might add—they were scheduled to leave for the Pioneer areas tomorrow afternoon. Tomorrow morning Prentiss would arrive at the detention center at eight o'clock sharp, give the incriminating holotape to one of Blacker's agents and have Violet released into his custody.

At least, that was the plan. But plans had a habit of going wrong, and her intuition told her that something was going to go very, very wrong...

"Maybe we should stay?" she said again, timidly.

"But, Mom!" Daisy exclaimed. "You've wanted to go Pioneer ever since I can remember!"

"Yes, Mom," Rose added. "Why the second thoughts now that everything's all set? Tomorrow Dad will bring Violet home and we'll all start a new life away from this—"

"Your mother is worried that everything might *not* go as planned," Prentiss cut in. "Am I right, Sunellen, honey?"

She sighed. Prentiss knew her too well. "I don't trust that scoundrel," she said softly. "Do you?"

"Not really, no," Prentiss said, giving her a hug. "But we're not going to let that stand in our way, are we?"

"Don't trust who?" Daisy and Rose asked in one voice.

Sunellen and Prentiss hadn't told the girls the truth about President Blacker, but it was time they did. When Prentiss explained about the plot to reduce oxygen in the Dome, Daisy and Rose were shocked.

"The dark side of politics, girls," Sunellen sighed. "Daisy, is your Knowing telling you anything?"

"No, Mom. Honest."

Not so honest, Sunellen thought. Daisy had never been a good liar. She knew something bad was going to happen but evidently she was not ready to say what it might be.

"She's worried about Pip," Rose explained. "That he'll escape to Outside or something."

Sunellen felt some relief. Not worried about *them*; just the dog! "That's highly unlikely, Daze," she said comfortingly. Ever since they'd started planning to go Pioneer, Daisy had made certain that Pip's microchip was securely in place. The alarm on the pouch in which he'd be carried and strapped to Daisy's chest was set to go off if even one of Pip's paws were to somehow get free.

Still, Sunellen couldn't shed her doubts about the whole Pioneer idea. Did she even have the right to ask her children to risk their lives by venturing into the unknown? Going Pioneer was, after all, basically a gamble. One *hoped* that conditions outside the Dome had improved to the point of sustaining life. But no one knew for sure. She thought often of her friend, Terra Brown, who'd left Blue Skies months ago with her husband and daughter, Calla; were they even alive? Or did they perish the moment they left the Dome's atmosphere?

Now she checked her wrist crystal. "It's nearly midnight. If we're really going to do this, I suppose we should finish packing."

They were allowed to take one suitcase each. Everything else—all the furniture in the apartment, dinnerware, utensils—must be left behind for the future tenants, whomever they might be. They were instructed to pack enough wafers and drinks to last for a week.

Sunellen had made sure to pack one of her most treasured possessions: The photo archive that showed the way things used to be on Earth before the treacherous Warming nearly destroyed the planet. Her mother had given her these photos—of trees and lakes and fields of wildflowers—and she had yearned her entire life to see these things for herself.

But now that her wish looked like it might come true, she was so unsure...

The strident alarm of a breaking news report interrupted her thoughts. Suddenly the walls of the apartment came alive with holographic images of the local news anchor, Vida Vassel, pointing behind her to an image of the S.T.E.P. Juvenile Hall of Detention:

"The transfer was said to have been made early this morning, by none other than Police Chief Clifford Mulligan himself," Vida said in her rapid-fire, staccato delivery. *"Although the 17th birthday of Violet Budd, the leader of the rebel group, TBT, is still days away, this station has learned that she has been removed from Juvenile Detention and taken to the adult prison in Sector 12."*

Sunellen froze. "Prentiss!" she screamed. "I don't understand...!"

"Neither do I," Prentiss said, rushing to her side, his face dark with anger. "Blacker! That devious Fossil Fueler! What does he think he's doing?!"

"Mom? Dad! What's happening?" Rose said, running to stand beside them.

Daisy joined them: "Dad? What does this mean—"

"I don't know what it means!" Prentiss replied more sharply than he intended.

The doorbell chimed. Once, twice, and then consistently. "Oh, no!" Sunellen gasped. "It's Blacker's men! He's double-crossed us! We're all being arrested!"

The doorbell kept ringing but no one moved; they stood frozen in place until, heart pounding, Sunellen finally found the courage to open the door.

When she did, she thought she must be dreaming, for there stood Police Chief Mulligan.

And standing right beside him, smiling her dazzling smile, was her daughter, Violet.

PART TWO: GOING PIONEER

Chapter 37

PRENTISS

"You don't have much time. He'll be sending his team here within the hour," Chief Mulligan told him. He seemed agitated, Prentiss thought, with his flushed cheeks and his eyes darting repeatedly to his wrist crystal. "You have to leave *now*! Everything's been arranged."

Sunellen had sent the girls to the bedroom to finish packing, their laughter a cheerful counterpoint to the circumstances of the moment.

"Cliff, I don't understand..." Prentiss began.

"You don't *have* to understand! I don't know all the details—my gut tells me you have something on him—but I've never seen Blacker so out of control! He gave the order to have Violet taken to adult prison and then, when you got down there to find out why, his agents are supposed to invade your apartment and search for..." he hesitated, shrugging. "...Something. He didn't bother to say what he was looking for. He simply told them to go over every inch of the place. Then he was planning to arrest you and 'throw away the key,' was how he put it."

Prentiss was stunned. "May I ask how you know all this?"

The Chief rolled his eyes. "Give me some credit, will you? I *am* the Chief of Police, after all. President Blacker's trusted ally, don't you know. Or at least I've convinced him that I am. I get all the news firsthand."

Sunellen put her hand on his arm. "Oh, Chief, aren't you taking a big risk coming here like this? How can we ever thank you?"

The Chief grinned sheepishly. "You can thank my wife, Augusta. She hates Drew Blacker as much as anyone." Turning to Prentiss he said, "She's forever grateful to you, Prentiss, for saving her life that time, and mine, too, when we had that awful virus thing. You could have reported us to a Relevance Lab, but you didn't." He added, "Besides, Augusta said if I didn't get Violet out of Juvey and help get your family to the Pioneer area, she'd serve me unflavored wafers for the rest of my life."

Prentiss was confused. "But—doesn't Blacker know that Violet isn't in prison? That you've disobeyed his orders and brought her here instead?"

"I've got that covered," Chief Mulligan said. "Two men on my staff were already in the process of bringing her in when I got to Juvey in time to take over. As far as Blacker is concerned, Violet's in a prison cell right now; he never checks. And when he does find out, probably in the morning, I'll simply say that the two idiots who were supposed to get her safely incarcerated, messed up. Lost her, or whatever. No one will believe them. Because I, as I've already pointed out, I am the Chief of Police!" He finished with a proud smile.

Prentiss' watch crystal pinged. He looked at it and then up at Chief Mulligan. "It's Blacker!"

"Answer it!" Chief whispered.

Prentiss did so, feigning righteous anger: "Blacker! What have you done?! I thought we had a deal..."

"We *do* have a deal!" Blacker insisted, sounding apologetic. "It's all been an unfortunate mistake! *Another* prisoner was supposed to be taken, not your daughter! Please forgive me, Dr. Budd. Why don't you come on down to the prison right now, and I'll get Chief Mulligan to release your daughter into your custody immediately!"

Prentiss breathed false relief. "Well, in that case..."

"Oh. And of course, you'll bring the...you know, what we agreed upon?"

"Of course," said Prentiss. When he hung up, Chief Mulligan was frantically pointing to his watch crystal.

"Now!" he said urgently. "We have to go *now*!"

As the Budd family was leaving their apartment for the last time, Prentiss slipped something into Chief Mulligan's pocket.

"What's this?" the Chief asked, fingering the slim, rounded object. "Feels like a holotape..."

"It's the key to the future of Blue Skies Dome," Prentiss said cryptically. "Vida Vassel at the news station will surely appreciate it. Make sure you get it to her right away."

Chief Mulligan nodded. "At your service, Dr. Budd. Always."

And that was how the Budd family began their journey: One night earlier than planned, with danger lurking at every turn, and not a nanosec too soon.

Chapter 38

DAISY

They left in such a hurry she'd almost forgotten to take Pip's pouch. She'd grabbed it off her bed mat at the last minute, and Violet had helped lock the straps in place, making sure that it fit snugly across her chest. Maybe too snugly? Daisy thought now, as Pip frantically kept trying to get himself free.

"Shhhh, Pippy, quiet down!" she whispered when he'd started to whimper. He did stop, for a nanosec, but then his paws started scratching against the PlasFabric pouch material again.

"Did you give him a Sleepet?" Rose asked.

Oh, no! She'd forgotten about the rule on the Pioneer application: *A dog or cat (one animal per family!) must be transported in an approved, locked pouch. A Sleepet tablet is recommended to keep the animal calm. Any dog or cat found to cause inconvenience to passengers will be prevented from further travel. The required pet fee of $5,000 is due at the point of departure.*

Her father had paid the pet fee without complaint—plus the fees for the rest of the family which were $10,000 per person. At least her father was able to ride for free as part of his Global Sustainment Prize for helping discover the cure for cancer. Still, it was a lot of money, and, in fact, Violet had made it one of her future crusades to allow anyone who wanted to go Pioneer to ride for free once the Dome was permanently opened.

She turned to Violet who was sitting next to her on the hover bus. "I'm so glad you're out of that horrible place, Vi!" she said, not sure if she could be heard above the constant drone of conversations swirling around them.

"Me too, Daze," Vi said, leaning close so that their foreheads touched. "I just hope this isn't a dream!"

The rows of narrow benches that filled the hover bus were not very comfortable, especially with the passengers so tightly crammed together, but Daisy guessed they were lucky to get seats at all. They hadn't been scheduled to leave until tomorrow, after all, and this bus was nearly full by the time Chief Mulligan got them to the departure area. "The driver's doing me a personal favor by squeezing you in," he whispered to her parents.

Squeezing was right, Daisy thought.

"Chief Mulligan, I don't know how to thank you!" her father had said before the bus took off.

Her mother gave the Chief a hug. "We'll never forget all that you've done for us!"

Daisy was surprised to see tears filling Chief Mulligan's eyes. He was such a burly, rough-looking character, but she should have known not to rely on outward appearances. She'd once thought Sharkey Collins had turned into a decent person until she learned that he would be working in a Relevance Lab, torturing animals.

It was hard to see anything by the light of the tiny sudoflickers that were embedded in the bus ceiling. They had been riding for two days now. At the moment, there was hardly any traffic on the Interdome Automation Highway. The buildings that lined both sides of the road slipped by quickly, dark, hulking shapes with nary a flicker in their tiny window slots. The buildings in Blue Skies Dome all looked exactly alike—tall, gray slabs with nothing to distinguish one from another except their numbered addresses. Daisy wondered what the buildings would look like when they arrived at their destination. *If there even were buildings. If they ever arrived...*

"I think we're headed east," said Rose, who was seated on the other side of her. "Is your Knowing telling you anything?"

It was odd, but for once, her "gift" was being stubbornly silent. The one time she would have liked to know what the future held—or even if there *was* a future waiting for them at the end of this trip—Daisy had no clue.

"Just the same scary thing about Pip," she told Rose. "That he'll escape to Outside..."

Pip, who had fallen asleep in his pouch, stirred at the sound of his name. He began to whimper again.

"Shhh," Daisy said, leaning close to the pouch. "He's probably hungry," she said to Rose. "I hope we—" She didn't have time to complete the sentence before a message came on the loudspeaker:

"Attention, passengers! We are now arriving at a transfer point. When you leave this bus you must await further instructions. There will be a half-hour rest period. You are strongly advised to have a meal and use the bathroom facilities. The next leg of your journey will consist of another full day."

The passengers, already tired and cranky after two days and nights, groaned. And that's when the unthinkable happened: One passenger, a woman who had been sitting two rows in front of them, seemed to snap: "This is all a hoax! There *is* no life outside the Dome! We're all going to die!!"

Pandemonium broke out as the other passengers stood and stumbled toward the exits of the bus. "What if she's right?" someone else yelled. "What if they're going to evaporate us the minute we get off this bus?"

The driver and some of the other passengers, Daisy's father included, tried to calm them but it was no use; people fell against one another in their rush to the exits, while others refused to budge, blocking their way.

Pip, frightened by all the noise, began to scratch frantically inside his pouch. He barked in a way Daisy had never heard: Loud and insistent, he sounded like a dog three times his size.

"Try to stay together," Daisy's father instructed her and her sisters. "Don't get trampled on!"

A wild-eyed looking man with bushy black hair fell against Daisy hard enough to jostle the straps on Pip's pouch. "Lemme out!" the man was screaming, "I don't wanna die! Take me back to the Dome!" he insisted.

And that's when Daisy heard the alarm: Pip's pouch had opened on one end! In another instant, the little dog had maneuvered his way free, and before Daisy or her sisters could stop him, he ran to the bus door and out of sight.

"PIP!!!!" Daisy yelled: "PIPPY! COME BACK!"

Violet, ever the heroine, pushed ahead through the crowd and chased after him. "Pip!" Daisy heard her call again and again. "Here, Pip, come back..."

Oddly enough, the episode seemed to have a calming effect on the other passengers. They quieted down and stared as Daisy, Rose and their parents elbowed their way off the bus. "We'll get him," Rose kept saying. "Don't worry, Daisy, he'll come back..."

Except that he didn't come back. When at last Daisy was able to elbow her way off the bus, she saw Violet, staring into the dark, unfamiliar distance. "Oh, Daze," Violet said. "I'm so very, very sorry!"

"It's all your fault!" Daisy sobbed. "You probably didn't lock the pouch straps tight enough! I hate you! I wish you were still in prison!"

"Daisy." Her mother had come up behind her. "Darling, that's not fair," she said softly.

"Maybe someone will find him and bring him back," Rose said. "You'll offer a reward..."

"Daisy, sweetheart, no one could have foreseen this," her father said.

But he was wrong. *She* had foreseen it. Her Knowing had warned her that this very thing would happen, but no one had believed her.

Chapter 39

ROSE

They ate their dinner wafers scrunched together at a long table, surrounded by strangers. The mood of the passengers had calmed considerably, with the hysterical woman and the bushy-haired man who had started all the ruckus being taken to—well, Rose didn't know exactly where.

Her father had examined them and told the bus driver that he thought they posed no real danger to anyone and, in his opinion, they should be permitted to continue on the trip if that's what they wanted. But evidently the driver didn't agree, and the disturbed passengers were escorted to another bus and that was the last anyone ever saw of them.

"Someone should check on Daisy," Rose told her mother after they'd finished their dinner. Daisy had wanted to be alone after Pip ran away, and at the moment she was sitting in the empty bus, sobbing as if her heart were broken, which it totally was.

"Would you, sweetie?" her mother said. "That would be so kind..."

"I'll go," said her father, standing up and grabbing a plate of dinner wafers. "I know she's upset, but she has to eat."

"It's my fault," Violet said miserably. "Maybe I *was* careless about locking the pouch straps..."

"It *wasn't* your fault," Rose said. "Don't you remember how Daisy was complaining that the straps were too *tight*?"

Violet sighed. "Maybe. But we'll never know for sure. And I don't think Daisy will forgive me. Ever."

They lapsed into silence. Rose looked around, trying to make sense of their surroundings. Sudoflickers mounted on tall poles outlined a nondescript courtyard encircled by parked hover buses. They were still under the Dome, of that she was certain; the high ceiling above them reflected no light whatsoever. Several yards to their left was the building that housed the bathroom facilities. She checked her wrist crystal: 3:00 a.m. The feeling that they could be anywhere and nowhere was unnerving.

"Hi, I'm Judson Lake," said a voice to her right. She looked up to see a lanky boy about her own age slip into the seat her father had occupied.

Slightly taken aback, Rose stammered, "I'm—I'm Rose. Budd. Do I know you?"

He smiled. She had to admit it was a cute smile: deep dimples in both cheeks. "You may not know me, but I sure know you. You're the person who gave Ellis Starr what she deserved."

Rose heard a soft giggle from Violet. "Your reputation precedes you," Vi said.

"Hey, I'm really sorry about your sister losing her dog," Judson said. "Will she be okay?"

Rose shrugged. "Eventually, I hope." She tried to remember if she'd ever met this boy before and couldn't. "Did we have any classes together?" she ventured. Not that it mattered. After losing her heart to Decker Bliss, she vowed never to care about any boy ever again.

"Advanced Physics, first year. I sat behind your boyfriend, Decker Bliss."

Rose winced. "He's not my boyfriend anymore," she said, unable to keep the sadness out of her tone.

"Good," she thought she heard Judson mutter under his breath.

"*Good?*" she repeated resentfully.

He gave her a direct look. "Yeah. He was basically a Domer. You know. Narrow-minded. As they used to say back in the day, 'uncool.'"

Back in the day? Rose thought. No one used that expression anymore.

As if reading her thoughts, he added, "I took Ancient Modern History with your mom, too." He leaned across Rose and said, "Hi, there, Mrs. Budd," to her mother.

"Hello Judson," said her mother, returning his smile. "Is your family here with you?"

He pointed toward the end of the long table. "Right there. My parents and my twin brother, Travis."

Her mother waved to them, and they waved back.

"You're a multiple?" Rose asked, stunned. How could she not have known them? *Because you were so totally involved with Decker you never noticed anyone else*, came the unspoken reply.

"Uh huh," Judson nodded. "I used to see you and your sister, Daisy, at the beach all the time." He pointed to a dessert wafer on her plate. "Mind if I have that one?"

"Go ahead," she said, feeling disconcerted. He seemed to know so much more about her than she did about him. But before she could say anything, a message came on the loudspeaker:

"Attention, Pioneer Passengers: Please line up in front of Bus 14. That's the black HoverPlus bus at the southern end of the courtyard. Be certain to take all of your belongings. As you enter the bus, you will each be given a pair of eyeshields and a small inhalator. Please be careful not to damage these items in any way, as you will not be permitted to exit the bus without them when we arrive at our destination."

"And where might that be?" Rose heard Violet whisper.

"Guess we'll know soon enough," Judson said. To Rose, he said, "Well, gotta get back to my family. See ya, Rose Budd."

"See ya," she said uncertainly.

"Oh, look, there's your father!" her mother exclaimed.

Rose looked up to see her father and Daisy walking toward them. Daisy's eyes were red and swollen, and she was still wearing Pip's empty pouch against her chest.

"Dad, did you hear the announcement?" Rose said.

"I did. So let's make our way to HoverPlus bus 14, shall we?"

Violet came up and reached for Daisy's hand. "How're you doing, Daze?"

Daisy pulled her hand away. "How do you think I'm doing?" she said, breaking into sobs again. "Poor Pip is probably so scared, so alone and lost!"

Rose hugged her. "Come on, Daze," she urged softly. "It's time to go."

And so they went: first Daisy and Rose, then her parents, and, trailing behind, Violet, who looked miserable and sad at a time when she should have been happier than ever before.

Chapter 40

VIOLET

She was back in Juvey and Glacier Starr was grabbing her arm and dragging her down the long, gray corridor. "Where are you taking me? I'm still 16!" she kept yelling but no sound would come out. They passed a cell where Clinker waved to her and another where Bloo was coughing, and yet another where Pip was chained to the bars, whimpering, his little tail tucked firmly between his legs...

"I'm still 16!" she yelled. She opened her eyes to see her mother leaning over her, her finger laid to her lips in a shushing gesture.

"Violet," her mother whispered, "wake up, honey. You were dreaming."

Violet's heart was pounding and for a moment she couldn't quite focus. "A nightmare," she breathed. "Horrible..."

Her mother gave her a soft kiss on the cheek. "It's okay, Vi," she said soothingly. "Settle down, darling, and try not to wake your sisters."

Violet looked to her left. Sure enough, Daisy and Rose sat huddled together, sound asleep. Even her father, in the adjacent row, was snoring softly. Looking around, she saw that most of the passengers were either asleep or looking as if they just woke up. Violet thought it must be very late, but her wrist crystal read 11:00 a.m.

How could that be? If it were mid-morning, wouldn't the simu-sun be shining? If it were overcast, there should at least be enough light to see *something*. But no matter how hard she peered through the bus windows, there was only darkness. No building shapes, no deviation of color to indicate they were passing...anything.

Were they in some sort of tunnel? It was very disorienting. She took a deep breath and looked around. This bus was much larger than the first one. Violet assumed that the "plus" in the HoverPlus bus referred to the bathroom facilities on board, so at least they wouldn't have to endure another stop.

She looked up. The weirdly shaped panels in the bus ceiling reflected nothing. Something was strange about the seats, too; they did not feel hard, like Neufab; and they weren't soft, like PlasFabric. Just—different.

Better get used to different, she told herself, getting to her feet carefully so as not to disturb anyone. "I need to use the bathroom," she whispered to her mother, who whispered back her customary "Be careful."

Violet eased her way through the rows of sleeping passengers, more than once nearly tripping over an extended leg or a piece of luggage left carelessly in the aisle.

She glanced at her image in the bathroom mirror and winced. In the pale glow of the sudoflickers, her complexion looked sallow and unhealthy. *The result of all that Juvey food,* she thought. She realized she had come perilously close to spending the rest of her life in prison. If Chief Mulligan hadn't rescued her—and if her father hadn't been so influential—she just might be...

Her thoughts were interrupted by a knock on the bathroom door. "Be right out," she said, opening the door to a woman and a little girl about six years old.

"Thank you," said the woman. And, "Do you know when we'll be getting to wherever it is we're going?"

Violet shook her head and smiled at the little girl. "Wish I did. But it can't be too much longer."

"Well, I hope you're right because we're running out of holobooks," the woman said in exasperation.

On the way back to her seat, Violet heard someone call her name. "Wanna sit here for a sec?"

It was the twin brother of that boy who talked to Rose in the courtyard at dinner yesterday. "I'm Travis," he introduced himself, patting the seat beside him.

Violet shook her head and whispered, "Sorry, I have to get back to my family..."

"Please?" he begged. "Just for a nano? Everyone's sleeping. I'm so bored. And I've been meaning to talk with you since I first saw you on the other bus."

She glanced down a few rows. Her sisters were still sleeping, and her mom, too. But her father had wakened and was watching her. He sent her a little wave that she returned, and reluctantly slid into the seat next to Travis.

"About what?" she asked. "What were you meaning to talk to me about?"

Travis smiled shyly. "I wanted to tell you that I think you did a really brave thing. With the Dome, I mean. Sorry you got into trouble for it."

"It could have been a lot worse," Violet said. "It *did* go a lot worse for my friends..." She thought of Clinker and Bloo and poor Palmer Davis and felt suddenly close to tears.

"I know how you must feel," Travis said. "Almost guilty to be going Pioneer."

She glanced at him. Travis looked nothing like his twin brother, Judson. They must be fraternal twins, Violet reasoned. Just as she and her sisters were fraternal triplets. "I do feel guilty," she admitted. "Though my father says guilt is almost always a misguided emotion."

"Your father is a great man," he said. "Guess the apple doesn't fly too far away from the tree."

She giggled.

"What's funny?" Travis wanted to know.

Her mother had used that ancient expression once or twice. "You mean, 'the apple doesn't *fall* far from the tree,'" she corrected.

"Great," Travis muttered. "That's what I get for trying to make an impression."

The thing was, Violet thought, he *was* making an impression. A very good one, too...

"I wonder what's out there in all that darkness?" she asked, peering out the bus window.

"If I had to guess, I'd say we're in the Outlying Flats."

Of course! She should have known! The Outlying Flats was the area that separated Blue Skies Dome from the Pioneer area; it was literally the edge of Outside. It was said to consist of vast stretches of vacant space, and she knew no one who had ever traveled this far!

Her thoughts were suddenly interrupted by a sudden, downward jolt of the bus. People were shaken awake and there were gasps all around.

"Violet!" her father called sharply from up front. "Over here! Now!"

"Go!" Travis said. "And don't be scared!"

"I'm not scared!" she lied, and ran to where her sisters and mother were now awake and waiting for whatever would happen next.

There was a series of chimes, similar to the chimes that sounded between classes at school. Then the loudspeaker came on:

"Attention, passengers! In a couple of nanosecs we will be approaching the Pioneer District to which you've been assigned. Please be sure to have your eye shields and inhalators at the ready. Do not leave any of your possessions behind."

Someone asked if they should remain seated.

"Yes! Don't move until I tell you!"

In the semidarkness of the bus, Violet felt Daisy's hand seek her own. "Vi, I'm really sorry for what I said. I didn't mean it! I love you! Please—I need you to forgive me before we die!"

"No one's going to die, Daze," Violet began. "And I do forgive—"

She was interrupted by a loud, grinding noise of metal scraping against metal. She knew that sound! It was the sound SumbraSteel made when the Dome was opened for a few nanosecs every Domes-Day!

"Eyeshields on, everyone!" ordered the driver. "If you feel yourself becoming lightheaded, use your inhalators! They will give you the extra oxygen you might need as we exit the Dome."

"Keep your eye shields on tightly, girls!" her father said, echoing the driver's instructions. "Don't remove them until I say it's okay!"

Violet involuntarily closed her eyes. She kept them closed even when she felt something cool and wispy blow against her skin. She kept them closed as a light bright enough to penetrate even the dark eye shields, filled her with its warmth.

"Okay, girls," her father said softly. "Open your eyes now, and take a look. Oh, my darlings, look!"

And so it was that on October 18, in the year 2275, as the watch crystal on her wrist pinged noon, Violet and her sisters removed their eye shields and beheld their future.

It was the precise moment they turned 17.

PART THREE: BLUE SKIES

Chapter 41

SUNELLEN

In all her imaginings, she had never pictured anything as heart-stoppingly beautiful as the scene before her: A sky so wide and expansive, yet so vibrant, the word "blue" did not do it justice. Below the sky the land was not monochrome gray the way it was in the Dome, but green with undulating rises and dips as far as the eye could see. Upon the land, in an intricate, evenly spaced pattern, stood hundreds—perhaps thousands—of slim white towers with rotating blades—wind turbines, she would learn.

"Oh, Prentiss!" she breathed. "I never—"

"I know," he said, his voice catching. "It's unbelievable."

She turned to him. She had never known Prentiss to be emotional, but now she swore those were tears glistening in his eyes.

"Welcome to New Connecticut!" A man was speaking from a staged area in front of a round building with transparent walls and roof. "You've had a long trip and we know you must be eager to get to your new homesteads, but first there are some formalities to get through. So if you would be kind enough to follow our guides into the building behind me, you will be given brochures that will answer many of your questions. After all the completed forms are collected, we will administer the Oath of Loyalty to Preserve Planet Earth, which is required of all Pioneers, adults and children. Then we will proceed to the dining area, where we have prepared a homegrown meal for you."

Murmurs of appreciation emanated from the crowd. Sunellen realized that she was, indeed, famished. The girls must be hungry as well; her beautiful daughters had turned 17 today! It was a good omen, she thought: A new year and a new start for, hopefully, a wonderful new life.

She turned to where Rose and Violet were taking in the scene with pure wonder shining on their faces. Only Daisy looked sad, and Sunellen couldn't really blame her. She loved Pip with all her heart, and the pain of losing him had robbed Daisy of taking pleasure in a life-changing moment.

They filed in slow, orderly procession into the transparent building, which was known as the Reception Depot. This was the first stop for all Pioneers who were assigned to New Connecticut, one of the states that had escaped major devastation when the Warming descended. Other cities and states to the east and south were not so lucky. New York, for example, whose wrecked skyscrapers were just visible on the far horizon, had resisted Doming until it was too late and was therefore determined to still be uninhabitable.

She knew that Rainbow Arc Dome, to the far north, still protected states like Vermont and Maine and a large section of Canada; Clearpoint View Dome covered much of the Midwest. Between them there were the Pioneer areas, or "free zones", where the land seemed to want to thrive…

The speaker introduced himself as Joe Perry, Chief Greeter of Pioneers. He was a genial, baldheaded man who had the skill to put everyone—or nearly everyone—at ease. Sunellen scanned the faces of the crowd and saw that there were still some who looked nervous and mistrustful. Most people, however, appeared relieved to find themselves safe and unhurt. And alive!

After filling out an endless succession of forms asking for the usual—names, ages, reasons for going Pioneer, etc.—they were asked to stand for the Oath of Loyalty to Preserve Planet Earth. There was a muted scraping of chair legs against a polished, gleaming tile floor. "Please repeat after me," said Mr. Perry:

"We, the Pioneers of New Connecticut, do solemnly promise to do our utmost to maintain the integrity of Planet Earth. We will nurture her natural resources and assist in the recovery of her rain forests and crops. We will keep her oceans clean and free of pollutants.

We will respect our planet by banning forever the use of fossil fuels or other harmful agents that contribute to the buildup of greenhouse gases in our atmosphere. We will keep our solar panels and wind turbines in top operating condition, and maintain the electrosynthesizers that keep our hydrogen fuel tanks running.

This we vow as Pioneers and good citizens of New Connecticut and the world."

There was silence as the meaning of these beautiful words sunk in.   And then people seemed to take a collective deep breath, and everyone began to embrace one another: families and strangers alike.

Sunellen had just one regret: That she and Prentiss and the girls hadn't gone Pioneer sooner, that they had wasted precious years under the suffocating atmosphere of Blue Skies Dome.

Chapter 42

PRENTISS

After they'd taken the Oath of Loyalty, and before they entered the dining area, one of the guides—a young man wearing a shirt emblazoned with the logo, "PIONEER PRIDE!" in large red letters—came to him with a request: "Excuse me, Dr. Budd? Mr. Perry asked if you would be kind enough to see him for just a moment."

For a nanosec Prentiss wondered how the guide knew who he was, but then he remembered the name tags that had been distributed with the packets of literature. He'd had a bit of trouble graviglueing his tag to his shirt, so Sunellen had helped, and the tag now rested, slightly askew, in the middle of his chest: "Prentiss Budd, DGH." The "DGH" stood for Doctor of Genomic Health, which was the standard medical degree for all practitioners in the 23rd century.

"Dr. Budd, welcome to New Connecticut!" Mr. Perry said, shaking his hand vigorously. "We feel so fortunate to have you with us!"

"I feel fortunate to be here," Prentiss said. It was true. He was still experiencing the slightly unreal feeling of unbelievable good luck. "How may I be of help to you, Mr. Perry?"

"Well, this is about the food we're about to serve. Because our homegrown fare is such a departure from what you're used to in the Dome—wafers and such..." —Mr. Perry grimaced at the word *wafers*—"...we occasionally have a bit of a problem." Here Mr. Perry hesitated. "You see, some folks have trouble..."

"...Digesting the new food?" Prentiss finished for him. "You mean—they vomit?"

Mr. Perry's face turned a deep shade of red. "Unfortunately—yes. They do vomit. Sometimes in abundance. It makes for a rather unpleasant experience for the other diners, if I may say so."

Prentiss nodded. *Unpleasant indeed*, he thought. "Have you considered offering a choice of wafers and asking people to try the new food a little at a time?" he asked.

"Oh, yes, of course!" Mr. Perry assured him. "It's even suggested in the New Food literature: 'For the health of your digestive system, please sample the homegrown food sparingly at first!' Trouble is, they mostly ignore the warning. When they see how luscious our vegetables and fruits look, most people chomp down like—well, as the ancient saying goes, like there's no tomorrow!"

"Understood," Prentiss nodded, unable to keep a smile from surfacing. "Do you want me to talk to them?"

Joe Perry's eyes closed in relief. "Oh, that would be wonderful," he breathed. "Everyone knows who you are. What you've done for mankind with the invention of Genocell. They'll be much more inclined to listen to you than to me."

And so it was that Prentiss offered his first medical service as a new citizen by urging people to eat the familiar wafers first, and introduce the homegrown foods to their digestive systems gradually.

This was met with a gruff-voiced man declaring, "If I wanted to eat wafers, I woulda stayed in Blue Skies!"

There was a sprinkling of laughter and a couple of "Yeah's" and pleas to "Give us the food already!"

He warned Sunellen and the girls to first eat a wafer or two to coat their stomachs with the familiar, and only then sample the carrots and tomatoes and wheat muffins.

"It's almost too beautiful to eat!" Rose said, staring at the gorgeous orange carrot on her plate. She took a bite and was surprised by the crunchy sound it made.

"Slowly!" Prentiss warned, watching her.

"Delicious!" she announced after a few more bites, offering the carrot to Violet.

"I have my own food!" Violet said, popping a slice of juicy red tomato into her mouth, her eyes closing with pleasure. "How did we ever convince ourselves that wafers were good?" she asked. "Compared to this, they're not worthy to be called 'food'!"

Daisy and Sunellen bit into their respective wheat muffins and murmured "Yum!" in unison. It was the first time Prentiss had seen Daisy smile—a true smile—since Pip escaped.

Now it was his turn. Prentiss decided to start with something called "corn on the cob"—a yellow cylinder type of vegetable he was told had just come into season and was growing in abundance all over New Connecticut.

The concept of "seasons" was as foreign to him as vegetables grown in real soil, coming from a place where there were neither. Nothing had been able to grow inside the Dome, no matter how hard the botanists had tried. SumbraSteel had filtered out the good along with the bad.

He took a bite of the corn and chewed. It had a strange, slippery quality. He decided to take another bite, a larger one this time. Suddenly—*oh, no!* he thought, getting quickly to his feet. He grabbed the little basin that had been distributed along with the plates. *Too much, too soon!* he thought as he turned away from his family. *Next time, take your own advice!* he admonished himself.

And while Prentiss would eventually come to relish and appreciate the incredible variety of vegetables and fruits that grew in their own backyard, he was never able to fully appreciate corn on the cob.

When the meal was over, people were asked to line up at an exit at the rear of the building where hovercycles would take them to their new homesteads.

As they left the building, they were greeted by a crowd waving "New Connecticut" banners and shouting, "Welcome, new citizens!" Some people recognized a few of the newcomers and broke from the crowd to embrace them.

Guides handed out tee shirts with the "PIONEER PRIDE!" logo in all different colors. Rose and Violet chose red; Daisy picked pale blue, a reflection of her feelings, Prentiss guessed. He and Sunellen both chose a vibrant yellow, like the sun, which was now shining with a softer, golden hue.

Prentiss checked his wrist crystal: Nearly five p.m. In October the sun wouldn't set before seven p.m. and it was still pleasantly warm. The Warming catastrophe had played havoc with the seasons all over the globe. Here in the Northeast, winter was now the shortest season, coming on toward the end of January and lasting only through the middle of February. They had landed in New Connecticut smack in the middle of a long autumn.

The brochure Prentiss studied while they waited for their hovercycle said the temperature during winter sometimes dipped all the way down to 65°F! It was an encouraging sign.   At the height of the Warming, temperatures of 125°F and higher had scorched a good part of the earth.   He was so absorbed in the literature that at first he didn't hear his name being called.

"Prentiss! Prentiss Budd!"

"Prentiss, look!" Sunellen said, jostling him with her elbow. "Isn't that—?"

He looked up to see someone running toward him. He blinked in the radiant golden light of the sun: *Bill?*" he gasped, his jaw dropping. "Bill Simmons?!"

"None other!" The two friends embraced, hugging and slapping each other happily on the back.

"When did you—how did you—" Prentiss began. He thought he might never again see his old buddy from medical school!

"About a month ago," Bill said, still hugging him. "I tried to holo-message you but that damned SumbraSteel..."

"I know, I know! Nothing gets through SumbraSteel!" Prentiss grinned, his heart still racing. "You remember Sunellen, don't you?"

"Of course I do!" Bill said, giving Sunellen a resounding kiss on the cheek. "Still beautiful as ever!"

"And you," Sunellen said, her cheeks flushing pink, "still the flatterer!"

"And these," Prentiss said, pointing to the girls who were frankly staring at this tall, ruddy-cheeked man with the booming voice, "These are my girls. My beautiful triplets, Rose, Violet and Daisy."

Bill Simmons smiled and shook his head in awe. "Beautiful is right," he said. "Beautiful flower girls. Welcome to your new life!"

Chapter 43
ROSE

Her father leaned over her bed and gave her a reassuring smile, but she wasn't fooled. She could see the concern in his eyes and that made her feel even worse. "What's wrong with me, Dad?" she asked in a voice she didn't recognize as her own.

"Sweetie, I'm not sure yet, but Bill Simmons will be here soon and together we'll get to the bottom of it. Try to rest."

Violet and Daisy stood in the doorway to their room—*her* room, she corrected herself; now that they lived in a house they each had their own room—and they looked scared. "You'll be okay, Rose. It's probably just something you ate," Violet said unconvincingly.

Rose didn't think so. It wasn't her stomach that hurt. It was—well, everything else. Her throat felt as though she'd swallowed a packet of cybernails; her ears thrummed like amplified sound waves, and, worst of all, she couldn't breathe! Something had evidently invaded her nasal cavity and blocked it—she wondered if it could have been one of those small winged creatures that inhabited this part of the world—the black things people called flies?

Her father had examined her with the genometer and could find no anomaly. Her organs were in good working order, although he said her lung contractions seemed a bit weaker than usual. Thankfully, no masses or tumors showed up under the electroscopic radiometer.

She had a slight fever. Plus, she *sneezed!* Sneezing was unheard of in Blue Skies Dome where the air was filtered and bacteria and allergies were a thing of the past. A sneeze made a horrible, head-crunching sound, and the first time it happened to her, two days ago, she was certain she was going to die.

"Do you think it's a virus, Dad?" Daisy asked from the doorway where she and Vi had been told to stand in case whatever ailed Rose was contagious. "Something like the kind Mom had back in the Dome?"

"Your mother didn't have a virus, Daisy," he said. What she had was a lack of oxygen. And that's certainly not the case here."

As if on cue, her mother came into the room holding a cup of tea. Real tea, not NevaTea, which wasn't tea at all, just a liquid conglomeration of chemicals. She loved real tea, but now she turned away. "No, thanks, Mom," she said. Then she sneezed—not once, not twice, but three times in a row!

"Oh, Prentiss, what *is* this?" her mother frowned, stepping back.

"I don't know, Sunellen," her father admitted. "Try to sleep until Bill gets here, Rose," he said.

She closed her eyes, but the details of the last three weeks crowded her brain.

That first night, the hovercycle had brought them to their new home in a neighborhood known as Woodmont-Upon-Atlantic. The house had been chosen for them by the N.C.S.C.—the New Connecticut Settlement Committee—because of its proximity to the Life Research Center where her father had a job waiting for him as Chief of DNA Redevelopment.

Her mother had been given a position at the local high school, teaching Ancient Modern History, the same subject she taught back in Blue Skies Dome.

"I can't believe this is all for just our family!" Rose had exclaimed in wonder as they went from room to room in the new house. Instead of a tiny apartment with narrow window slots that looked out upon rows and rows of identical apartment buildings, they now lived in a home overlooking the Atlantic Ocean! It was a round structure with solar panels in the ceiling that let in beautiful, unsimulated light. The walls were made of laminated wood—real wood, not junky NeuFab. After the tsunamis and droughts had killed most of the trees on Earth, Pioneer scientists in this part of the world were able, over the course of many years, to harvest a few remaining seedlings. From these, they developed a laminate coating that could restore weakened wood to its former strength. Her father said the coating invention was a miraculous feat, as important to humanity as finding the cure for cancer.

Rose sneezed again. She sat up, extracted a tis-tab from the magnabin on her bed table, and wiped her nose. When she was done, the tis-tab evaporated with a comforting little *hsssss* sound and she lay back down on her pillow. She was still not used to sleeping on a real bed instead of a mat on the floor, but she was getting better at it. She'd fallen out of bed only twice in the past week, while Daisy had fallen four times and Violet not at all. She felt so sorry for Daisy, who was still having horrible nightmares about Pip.

Poor Pip, Rose thought. He was probably dead by now, which would be a good thing if he'd been captured and taken to a Relevance Lab. She couldn't believe there were no Relevance Labs here in New Connecticut, or in any other Pioneer area, or so she'd been told.

"Here, *everyone* is relevant as long as they're dedicated to restoring our planet," said Skyla Tor, her new friend from T.F.T. Academy, where Rose was enrolled as a freshman. T.F.T. stood for Teachers For Tomorrow, and to her delight, she'd been enrolled there by the Settlement Committee.

That was the purpose of all those forms, she thought now. *So they could learn about our interests and goals and know where we would be happiest and do the most good for our world...*

She finally dozed off, and when she woke her father and Bill Simmons were talking softly near her bedside.

"What's wrong with me, Dad?" Rose asked weakly.

The men turned to her. Her father tried to smile, but Bill Simmons wore a serious expression. "I'm afraid you have a cold," he said.

"But I'm *not* cold," she insisted. "Actually, I'm rather warm..."

Her father shook his head. "No, Rosie, not *cold*. I mean, you have a cold. A common cold."

Had her illness affected her mental ability? What was her father talking about—she *wasn't* cold, but she *had* a cold?

At her puzzled expression, her father leaned closer and took her hand. "Rose," he began gently, "this is something we haven't seen for centuries. It's called "common" because long ago, before the Warming, people got sick with it all the time. It's caused by a virus." He paused and glanced at Bill Simmons, who nodded. "Unfortunately, honey, there's no cure. Not yet, anyway."

Rose felt hot tears well up behind her eyelids. After all they'd been through, after barely escaping Domed existence and arriving here, in New Connecticut, she,

Rose Budd, was sick and would probably die. *It wasn't fair!*

"It's not fatal," Bill Simmons assured her. "It's just—well, a cold can be mighty uncomfortable. And it's contagious, so your sisters will probably get it, too. And maybe even your parents," he added, glancing at her father.

She opened her eyes and looked carefully at him. "You mean—I'll live?"

Bill Simmons smiled. "Yes, of course," he said. "In a few days, you'll feel good as new."

As they left the room, Rose heard her father say, "I'm going to get to work on this cold virus mystery right away, Bill. It can't be that tough to crack, can it?"

"Many have tried," Bill sighed. "And all have failed..."

A few minutes later, her mother brought her a cup of tea, which, this time, Rose gratefully accepted. "There's someone here to see you," her mother said, smiling, as Judson Lake appeared in the doorway.

It turned out that Judson and his family had been given a homestead just a mile down the road from their own. More coincidentally, he was also enrolled as a freshman at T.F.T. Academy, and they even shared a few classes together.

"Hi," he said, shyly. "Welcome to the real, unsimulated world of Pioneer, where ancient viruses still lurk."

I must look horrible, was Rose's first thought. But there was nothing she could do about that, so she shrugged. "My father's going to find a cure for this," she said, and was immediately embarrassed by how ridiculous that sounded. "Or at least he's going to try," she amended.

"Brought this for you," Judson said, handing her a red rose. She supposed he'd plucked it from one of the rose bushes that grew in front of their house. "Careful of the thorns..."

"It's beautiful," Rose said, bringing the flower to her nose where, because of her cold, she couldn't smell a thing. She'd heard that scientists had tried to breed a thornless rose but were unable to succeed. She was glad about that. A rose with no thorns would be unable to protect itself. It would be a bland, defenseless thing, a rose unworthy of the name.

Better to have a thorn or two, she thought with a smile, to defend against the Decker Blisses and Ellis Starrs of the world.

Chapter 44
VIOLET

She had never seen anything quite so beautiful. The tomato, which she held in the palm of her hand, was perfect in its roundness, and red as the sun that rose above the ocean each morning. The first time her family had watched the sunrise from their back porch, her mother had wept. "It's just as my mother described it to me, and my grandmother described it to her, only—only more beautiful!" her mother said, tears sliding down her cheeks as they watched the dark sky slowly turn magenta, then pink, and finally pale blue.

"Before the Warming this wasn't an ocean," her father explained. "It was merely an inlet, or a bay of some sort. I think they called it Long Island Sound."

"What sort of a sound did it make?" Daisy wanted to know.

"I'm not sure," her father replied. "In any case, all the land in this area was submerged beneath the rising tides until, about 50 years ago, the water levels started to recede." He looked at them: "It's in the literature we received when we arrived here. You should be studying it; this is our home now. Learn as much as you can about it."

"Excellent idea!" her mother said. "I'll be giving you a pop quiz by the end of the week."

Violet and her sisters groaned, but they knew her parents were right. The more familiar they became with the history of their surroundings—of New Connecticut and the other Pioneer areas that were scattered between the Domed cities like oases in a vast desert—the better equipped they would be to help with the Recovery.

Now Violet popped the beautiful tomato into the basket she held to collect vegetables for their dinner. In addition to their regular jobs and student responsibilities, Pioneer families were responsible for cultivating their own gardens. Along with the tomatoes that were ripening nicely on their wooden stakes, there was lettuce, yellow squash and a leafy vegetable called Swiss Chard.

And the flowers! The family who previously lived in their homestead—Violet heard they had relocated further east to a Pioneer area called Bostonia—had planted flowers of every imaginable kind.

There was a meadow on the south side of their house that was filled with orange tiger lilies, blue iris, yellow and white daisies, and, yes, even her namesake flower, purple violets—the exact color of her eyes, her mother insisted.

She had to admit she secretly preferred the violets to the other flowers; although they were small and appeared fragile, they grew in abundance even where the soil was still sparse, and their fragrance was sweet but not cloying.

"Dinner will be ready soon," her mother said when Violet came inside. "Are you feeling better, Vi?"

"Much," she said. She'd been the second triplet to take to her bed with the horrible cold virus. Now poor Daisy had it; she could be heard sneezing and coughing in her room.

"Would you like me to take Daisy some tea?" Violet offered.

"Yes, please," her mother nodded. "And bring her a tomato, too. Dad thinks they might contain vitamin C."

"Sure hope he can cure this plague," Violet said, shuddering.

"He's giving it his all," said her mother. "If anyone can cure the common cold, your father can."

Daisy didn't want tea or anything else. "I'm dying," she groaned. "Go away."

"You're not dying, Daze," Vi assured her, but she honored her wish to be miserable alone.

Back in her own room, Violet thought about yesterday when she and Rose had gone to the Reception Depot to welcome the new Pioneers. It wasn't required, but Violet thought it would be a nice thing to do as a way to show their appreciation for all they'd been given here in New Connecticut.

Besides, there was always the possibility that someone you knew would be arriving from Blue Skies Dome...

The lack of communication between the Pioneer areas and their former home was frustrating. Here she was, breathing unpolluted air, eating real food, going to school—she'd been admitted to the prestigious New Connecticut campus of the Law Academy of the Northeast—while her old friends were—well, she didn't know how they were. Or even if they were still alive.

Were Bloo and Clinker still in jail? At times she was unable to sleep because of her feelings of guilt at leaving them behind.

Only yesterday they'd met someone from Blue Skies: "Look, Violet!" Rose said as they distributed "PIONEER PRIDE!" shirts to the newcomers. "Isn't that Mr. Jagger?!"

"It is!" Violet exclaimed. "Mr. Jagger! Mr. Jagger— over here!"

Mr. Jagger, who'd taught Ancient Music at Blue Skies High—who'd held Ellis Starr's wig in his hands after Rose had pulled it off in their scuffle—waved and flashed a smile of recognition. "Hello, Budd girls!" he said when they rushed up to him. "There was a rumor you and your family had gone Pioneer, but I couldn't be sure..."

"No one ever knows for sure," Rose said, shaking her head. "But now you know! And isn't it great?"

Mr. Jagger looked around. "It's—I'm—speechless!" he exclaimed.

Violet knew she shouldn't ask—the poor man was probably weary and overwhelmed by his long trip and new surroundings—but she couldn't help herself: "Mr. Jagger? Is there anything new back in Blue Skies?"

"New? You wouldn't believe how much is new! Did you know they arrested President Drew Blacker for corruption?"

Violet and Rose exchanged glances. "We did hear a rumor about that," Violet said. "But—what I mean is—have you heard anything about my friends Bloo Sycamore or Clinker James?"

Mr. Jagger looked sorrowful. "No, I'm afraid not. There's been some talk about opening the Dome permanently since Blacker's arrest, but so far—"

"...It's still only talk," Violet finished for him. She felt the familiar anger rise within her.

Just then Joe Perry, the Greeter of Pioneers, made an announcement asking the new arrivals to enter the building behind him, where they would take the Oath of Loyalty. "After that, we've prepared a meal for you." said Mr. Perry.

"Go easy on the homegrown food," Rose advised Mr. Jagger.

"We're in an area called Woodmont-Upon-Atlantic—about two miles from here," Violet said. She pressed the message relay button on her wrist crystal until it connected with Mr. Jagger's and then she holoscribbled their address. "Please come and visit us when you're settled," she said. My mom and dad will be so happy to see you."

"I'd love to," Mr. Jagger said. Then, "Wait—speaking of your family: Where's your sister, Daisy?"

"She's home with a—" Violet thought better of telling him about the rampant virus that had no cure. "She wasn't able to come today." Before he could reply, she offered Mr. Jagger his choice of a PIONEER PRIDE! shirt. He chose a purple one. The same color as her favorite flower.

Chapter 45

DAISY

Three things would happen to Daisy Budd at the end of December, almost three months after their arrival in New Connecticut. Three things that would change the course of her life:

The first thing...

This had to be a dream. She was sitting on the glider—*glider, what a wonderful word*! she thought—on the back porch, letting the sun warm her upturned face. Now that her cold was getting better and she could breathe again, she could smell the clean, ocean air. She'd made sure to douse herself with RaySpray to ward off what her father said were harmful effects of the sun, but privately she wondered how something that felt so good could also be harmful...

Her eyes closed and when she opened them she saw Pip. He was right there, at her feet, his tail wagging lazily against the laminated wood of the porch floor...

"Daisy? Are you awake? Daisy? It's me..."

Daisy opened her eyes and jumped up: "CALLA!" she screamed. The dog at her feet yelped in surprise. "Calla Brown!" she repeated. "Am I dreaming? Are you real?" The disappointment that the dog she thought might be Pip was Digger, his littermate, was overshadowed by the joy of seeing her best friend.

The girls hugged and jumped up and down excitedly.

"Am I real? That's like what I asked when we found Digger and Pip that day in Blue Skies, remember?" Calla said. "We'd never seen real dogs before, and I wasn't sure—" She stopped abruptly. "Oh, Daisy, I'm so sorry about Pip. Your mom told me—"

Daisy tried hard to suppress them, but the tears came anyway.

"Oh, Daze, don't," Calla begged.

"Sorry," Daisy sniffled, and forced a smile. "Calla, I've missed you so much! You look—great!" This was a lie. There was a sadness lurking in her friend's eyes that hadn't been there before. Now the Knowing was telling Daisy that something bad had happened in Calla's life. In another instant she knew what it was but she would wait for Calla to tell her.

The two friends sat down next to each other on the glider. "My parents have separated," Calla began as Digger jumped up between them, his little white tail wagging like mad.

Daisy ran her fingers through his soft fur the way she used to do with Pip. "I'm really sorry to hear that," she said. She listened as Calla told her how her family had originally been assigned to a Pioneer district in Australia. There, her father, a marine biologist, had been analyzing the waters of the Great Barrier Reef where coral was said to finally be regenerating after it had been destroyed by the Warming.

"He met someone there," Calla said softly. "Another researcher...a woman..."

Daisy slipped her arms around Calla's shoulders. "You don't have to tell me..."

Calla sighed. "I'm sort of okay with it now, Daze. Anyway, my mom applied for a teaching position back in this area, and guess what—she'll be teaching at the same school as your mom!"

As if on cue, they heard the sound of their mothers' mingled laughter coming from inside the house.

"Precious planet, my mom must be ecstatic!" Daisy said. "She missed your mother as much as I've missed you..."

The two friends spent the rest of that afternoon reminiscing. Daisy told Calla about Sharkey Collins and what a jerk he turned out to be, getting a job in a Relevance Lab where he was probably torturing animals. She told her about Rose's finally growing a spine and practically knocking out Ellis Starr, who was actually bald. She told her that Rose liked a boy named Judson Lake, and that Violet liked his twin brother, Travis, although she refused to admit it. She told her that Violet was already planning a protest drive to get all the Domes opened permanently.

"Some things change a lot," said Calla wistfully, "and other things never do..."

The next morning, when Calla crystal-called her to say she'd caught Daisy's cold and that she'd never forgive Daisy for making her feel so miserable, Daisy knew she didn't mean it. She knew without a doubt that whatever might happen between them, good or bad, she and Calla Brown would remain best friends all the days of their lives.

The second thing...

She finally knew what she wanted to be when she grew up. What she *didn't* want to be was a food consultant. Daisy didn't blame the Settlement Committee for enrolling her in a Food Management Training course at the local community college. On all the forms she'd filled out when they'd first arrived in New Connecticut, she'd listed her ambition to work at a Food Center because she wanted to improve the quality of wafers. But that was back in the Dome, where real, homegrown food was unknown. Here in beautiful New Connecticut, where they never had to endure another tasteless wafer, her ambition didn't apply.

Which left her feeling directionless and confused. Until one day, not long after reuniting with Calla, her father suggested she accompany him to the Life Research Center where he was working on the DNA Restoration Project.

"I thought you'd like to see where I spend most of my waking life," her father said dryly. Besides his regular work on the Restoration Project, he'd begun to stay late at the lab several nights a week, trying to find a cure for the common cold.

In the decades before the Warming, scientists around the world had been wise enough to extract and preserve DNA from almost every animal and plant species on Earth. Some of this preserved DNA was stored in tanks at the Life Research Center, where it was being used to repopulate the most devastated areas worldwide—Africa, where zebra and lions and gazelles had gone extinct, and Antarctica, where penguins and seals had died out when the ice shelf melted. It was the most important project her father had ever been involved with and his excitement was palpable. As they walked between the tall rows of storage tanks that held so much possibility for potential life, Daisy could understand why.

Stopping suddenly and turning to face her father, she burst out: "I want to be a scientist, Dad!" Her heart swelled with pride for all the good her father was doing. "I want to be just like you!"

So it was that she applied and was accepted to The New Connecticut School of Medical and Biological Sciences. She would have to make up a few science and chemistry requirements before she could be officially enrolled, and it might take six months or even a year, but she would do it!

Violet had her law school and political ambitions; Rose, a natural teacher, would have her career in education. And now she, Daisy, would do what she realized she'd always wanted to do: Bring animals back to beautiful life on Earth.

The third (and best) thing...

She would have liked to accompany Rose and Violet when they went down to the Reception Depot. It was fun to greet the new Pioneers and make them feel welcome, and there was always the chance they'd meet someone they knew from Blue Skies Dome.

"I can't," she'd told her sisters, pointing to the chemistry holotext she was studying. Although she'd taken some advanced chemistry classes in high school, she was finding college chemistry to be on a whole different—and difficult—level.

"She's no fun anymore," Daisy heard Violet complain to Rose as they ambled down the road toward the Depot.

"I know. She reminds me of Dad when he gets involved with a project," Rose said. "All work and no time for anything else..."

Daisy sighed and turned her face to the sun. On the porch, she'd erected a studynook to shield her from any distractions—no sound could penetrate it so she wouldn't be tempted to watch the waves as they rolled onto the shore—but she could still see the sun glinting through the trees, the puffy clouds as they drifted lazily against the blue sky...

Daisy! Concentrate! she admonished herself, turning to the chemistry formulas that surrounded her on all sides.

She lost all sense of time. When she finally switched off the hologram and extinguished the studynook, the sun had moved a good deal to the west. It would be dark soon. Daisy stood and stretched. She knew that her mother would be staying late at school tonight to grade exam papers, but what was keeping her sisters? They should have returned from the Reception Depot by now. She resented the fact that she would have to be the one to start dinner...

She paused in her thoughts when she heard someone calling her name.

As she left the porch she turned toward the road that led to town. Three figures loomed in the distance.

"Daisy! Daisy Budd!" someone called. Not her sisters; someone who was walking between them...

She strained to see who it was, but the sun's glare was blinding. She walked a bit farther, toward the field of flowers that grew on this side of the house.

Her heart began hammering wildly inside her chest. It couldn't be—*"Sharkey Collins?!?"* she called out, dumbfounded. "What're you...."

And then she noticed movement in the field of flowers: Something small, something with white triangular ears and a white tail was darting between the rows of wild red roses and blue iris and yellow daisies...

"PIP! PIPPY!" she shouted, her sobs nearly choking the words. "Here, boy! Here my darling! Oh, Pip!"

Daisy shouted as the little dog leapt into her arms and buried his head in her neck the way he always used to.

And then Sharkey was there, shaking his head, arms on his hips. "So you thought I was torturing animals, huh?" he said in an offended tone.

"I—I—" Daisy stammered. She looked at her sisters for help, but all they did was shrug with an expression that said: *That's what you thought, and that's what we told him.*

"I only took the job at the Relevance Lab so I could *save* the animals," Sharkey said. "When that crazy Ellis Starr brought Pip to the lab, I knew he had to be your dog because she found him near your old apartment. I guess he tried to find his way home after he escaped the hover bus. So I brought him to *my h*ouse until my Pioneer application was accepted. My father wasn't too happy, I can tell you."

"I think an apology is in order," Violet said.

"I think so, too," Rose echoed.

Daisy did apologize. She apologized right then and there, and kept the apologies coming through dinner and afterward. And later, when she offered to walk Sharkey to his new homestead that was just half a mile from their own, she apologized yet again: "Please forgive me, Sharkey. I am so sorry for misjudging you. I don't know how I can ever make it up to you for rescuing Pip."

"Oh, I guess I can think of a few ways," he said with a grin. They were passing through the field of flowers and Pip scampered ahead, making the rows of daisies sway in the moonlight. As Sharkey's homestead came into view, he stopped suddenly and pulled her close:

"Good night, Daisy Budd," he said, kissing her.

"Good night, Sharkey Collins," she whispered.

Sharkey kissed her again. "See you tomorrow?" he said.

"See you tomorrow," she replied.

As she watched Sharkey go inside, the Knowing was telling her that winter would be coming on soon. She was looking forward to the new season. She was looking forward to many things, wonderful things she was certain the future held in store. For her and Sharkey. For her family. For the whole new world to come.

"Come on, Pip," she said, shivering a little. "It's getting chilly."

The little dog barked his approval, his white ears and tail glistening like talismans as they made their way back home through the field of flowers.

Made in the USA
Lexington, KY
02 April 2013